The Moments

I'll Never Forget

LAUREN NORLEY

First published by Lauren Norley, 2025
Copyright © 2025 by Lauren Norley

All rights reserved. No part of this publication may be reproduced, stored or transmitted in any form or by any means, electronic, mechanical, photocopying, recording, scanning, or otherwise, without written permission from the publisher. It is illegal to copy this book, post it to a website, or distribute it by any other means without permission.

This novel is entirely a work of fiction. The names, characters and incidents portrayed in it are the work of the author's imagination. Any resemblance to actual persons, living or dead, events or localities is entirely coincidental.

Lauren Norley asserts the moral right to be identified as the author of this work.

Lauren Norley has no responsibility for the persistence or accuracy of URLs for external or third-party Internet Websites referred to in this publication and does not guarantee that any content on such Websites is, or will remain, accurate or appropriate.

Designations used by companies to distinguish their products are often claimed as trademarks. All brand names and product names used in this book and on its cover are trade names, service marks, trademarks and registered trademarks of their respective owners. The publishers and the book are not associated with any product or vendor mentioned in this book. None of the companies referenced within the book have endorsed the book.

First edition

ISBN (Kindle): 978-1-7641930-2-3
ISBN (Paperback): 978-1-7641930-1-6
ISBN (Hardcover): 978-1-7641930-3-0

This book was professionally typeset on Reedsy
Find out more at reedsy.com

Dedication

For my mum

I am the woman I am today because of you.

Your constant love, strength, and guidance have shaped every part of me.

Thank you for always standing beside me, even through the toughest chapters of my life.

This book is for you.

Acknowledgment

To my beautiful sisters and cherished family, thank you for your unwavering encouragement, your honest feedback, and for believing in this story even when I doubted myself.

And to my best friend, your constant presence in my life has been a source of joy and strength. Your friendship reminds me daily that I never have to face anything alone.

To my incredible husband, thank you for your boundless patience, quiet support, and for holding space for me while I poured my heart into these pages. Your belief in me means more than I can ever express.

To my parents, thank you for always telling me that anything is possible if you just work hard enough. Your words have stayed with me every step of the way.

To my amazing children, thank you for being my greatest inspiration and daily reminder of what truly matters. May you always chase joy, live boldly, follow your dreams, and know that anything is possible. Never forget how deeply you are loved.

This book wouldn't exist without all of you. From the bottom of my heart, **thank you.**

Contents

Through loss and grief, a new kind of love is found—one that heals, rebuilds, and redefines everything.

Chapter 1
The Moment That Changed Everything

As I lie here staring at the clock, watching the numbers flick over—2:01 a.m., 2:02, 2:03—I can't stop thinking about the moment that changed everything. Tears stream from my eyes onto the pillow, soaking a patch beneath my cheek.

If only I'd gone with them. If I hadn't chosen to stay home with Zeke… I'd be with them right now. Not lying here alone.

Just two months ago, we were celebrating my eighteenth birthday. In true rich-people fashion, my parents threw the biggest, fanciest party imaginable. Everyone we knew showed up. I wore a little black dress that hugged tight in all the right places, and I made sure not to drink too much—I wanted to remember the night forever. It was perfect. I danced, laughed with my friends, and fell asleep in the early hours, knowing it was a night I'd never forget.

Before the music faded and the guest left, Mum stood and tapped her champagne flute with a spoon. "One last toast," she said, her eyes shining. "To our daughter, our light, our wild heart—Lucy."

Dad raised his glass. "We always knew you were meant for big things. Whatever you dream, we believe in it. And we believe in you."

They clinked glasses, and I remember thinking how proud they looked. How safe I felt. How completely loved.

It was the last big memory I have of the three of us, all together. And it's one I'll never forget.

Three weeks later—Saturday, April 10th, to be exact—Mum and Dad had a fundraiser to attend. Normally, I would've gone with them. It was at the Harbourview, one of those charity galas they were always invited to. Sparkling dresses, clinking champagne, polite small talk masked behind big donations. Mum would've picked out a dress for me, and Dad would've made some cheesy comment like, "You'll outshine the chandelier, Lucy."

But that night, I didn't go.

I wanted to stay home with Zeke.

We'd been dating a few months, and I'd started thinking about taking things to the next level. Zeke and I started as close friends. He was sweet, reliable, safe—the kind of guy you could trust. But not the kind who made your stomach flip just by looking at you. Still, I cared about him. Part of me wanted to believe that what we had was enough.

That night, lying in bed with him, things started to heat up. It felt familiar… but not quite right. It didn't feel like a moment I'd never forget—and it should have.

When his hand slid up under my skirt, I froze. My breath caught. And then, before I could even think, the words tumbled out:

"No, please stop. I've changed my mind."

Zeke immediately pulled back. His eyes met mine.

"Hey… it's okay, Lucy," he said softly, brushing a strand of hair from my face. "You never have to do anything you're not ready for."

I let out a shaky breath I didn't realise I'd been holding. He didn't act hurt. Didn't get annoyed. He just lay beside me quietly and turned on the TV. He may not have been the one, but in that moment, he did the right thing.

It felt like I'd only just fallen asleep when I was jolted awake by pounding on the front door. A sound so loud it shook the glass panels. A sound that sent shivers down my spine.

I looked at the clock—11:48 p.m.

Heart racing, I jumped out of bed and rushed downstairs. I already knew something was wrong. No one knocks like that unless it's bad.

From halfway down the stairs, I could see through the glass— two police officers. Full uniform.

My chest tightened.

I opened the door. They stepped inside. And in that instant, the world stopped.

The female officer opened her mouth, but I couldn't hear anything over the thumping in my ears. She paused when she saw the look on my face, then gently placed a hand on my shoulder.

"Lucy, did you hear me? There's been an accident. Your

parents didn't survive."

I dropped to the floor.

Tears fell freely as my head shook in disbelief. Just hours ago, they were fine.

If only I'd gone with them…

As if reading my mind, the officer responded quietly, "Lucy, if you had been in the car, it wouldn't have made a difference. Except you wouldn't be here now."

Those words stuck with me. Because if I had gone with them, I wouldn't be here. I wouldn't be lying awake, alone, replaying every moment.

In the days that followed, the house was filled with people—friends, extended family, all offering condolences. Most brought food. I don't know why lasagna and casseroles became the universal "sorry your loved one died" dish, but they did.

And with the last condolence hug, the noise disappeared. Just like that, the funeral ended, the doorbell stopped ringing… and the house fell silent.

Painfully silent.

The funeral was a blur—black dresses, murmured condolences, people I barely recognised hugging me like they knew me. Everyone was saying the same things. "They were so proud of you." "They loved you so much." "They're watching over you now.

It didn't help.

The only part I remember clearly was Sienna.

She showed up in a simple navy dress, hair tied in a braid over one shoulder. No makeup. No theatrics. Just her—solid, quiet, real.

When I couldn't move from the bathroom floor that morning, she was the one who helped me get dressed.

When I couldn't eat, she handed me a glass of water and sat beside me, legs crossed like we were thirteen again and hiding from our parents during a sleepover.

And when their caskets were lowered into the ground and my knees buckled, she caught me before I hit the dirt.

She never left my side.

After everyone had gone, after the last casserole had been covered and the last chair stacked away, Sienna stayed behind. She helped me out of the itchy black dress and into my pyjamas. She ordered Thai food, and I barely touched it. Then she curled up at the foot of my bed, her hand resting lightly on my ankle—like she just needed to know I was still there."

Neither of us said much that night. But we didn't have to.

It was so quiet I could hear every leaf brushing against the windows. Every bird call. Every creak in the floorboards. And every thought in my head.

Words on repeat like, "You're lucky you're eighteen—you can keep the house."

"At least your parents left you well provided for."

But that's not luck.

Sure, I don't need to worry about bills. But I'd trade it all to have them back. I'm barely eighteen—I don't know how to be an adult. I barely know how to live without them.

I replay every decision from that night like it might change something. If I hadn't stayed with Zeke, if I hadn't been selfish, if I had just gone with them… maybe they'd still be alive.

And speaking of Zeke, I haven't seen him since the funeral. Maybe he's thinking what I'm thinking. Maybe he blames himself, too. Maybe he wonders if, by wanting me to stay, he helped seal their fate.

I can't bring myself to contact him. I know that looking at him would bring it all rushing back.

The clock flicks again—3:54 a.m., 3:55, 3:56… Sienna is now asleep at the end of my bed.

My eyelids finally grew heavy. Sleep wins.

Chapter 2

The Beginning I Didn't See Coming

I stand by the window, holding a cold mug of coffee I never actually drank. Outside, the world still looks the same. It's just kept spinning, it's like the world didn't stop two months ago.

But mine did.

My phone **buzzes** from the kitchen bench. Another message from someone I haven't had the energy to reply to. I used to care about friends, social invites, clothes, appearances, and plans. Now I barely care if I've brushed my hair.

Grief strips you bare. And what's left? Just the silence. The guilt. The aching 'what ifs' that curl around your ribs like vines.

I haven't been outside—really outside—since the funeral. Groceries get delivered. Meals arrive in cling wrap with little notes. "Thinking of you." "Let us know if you need anything." I never reply. What would I even say?

But today, something shifts. Maybe it's the unbearable quiet. Maybe it's the scent of Mum's perfume still lingering in the hallway. Maybe it's just the fact that I'm tired of staring at these four walls, waiting for the ache to fade.

It doesn't fade. But maybe if I move, if I just... go somewhere, it might feel a little lighter, even for a minute.

I throw myself together—pulling my long brown hair into a

messy knot, brushing a little mascara under my brown eyes—and grab my bag. Mum's locket rests against my chest—always there, a quiet reminder of her love. I've worn it every day since she gave it to me.

Then I head out, forcing myself to walk aimlessly down Main Street of our small country town.

And then—**splat**.

A blob hits my shoulder.

No. No. No. You have got to be kidding me.

I look down at my white shirt. A bird. A freaking bird just shit on me.

Of course. My first trip outside in months, and this is what I get.

I groan, digging through my purse for tissues, paying zero attention to where I'm going—and that's when it happens.

Hot, burning liquid splashes across my chest. I yelp in pain and shock.

Now I'm standing in the middle of the street, soaked in coffee. Bird shit and coffee? Really? In the same five minutes?

I glance up, furious, and then I see him.

He's tall—definitely taller than me—with short brown hair that looks like he ran his fingers through it instead of using a comb, and warm brown eyes that hold a flicker of panic. He's got just enough muscle to look like he works out but doesn't obsess over it.

And somehow, even as he's apologising, I can't stop staring while he is holding an empty coffee cup, looking horrified.

"Oh my God, I'm so sorry," he says, pulling a handkerchief from his pocket and dabbing at my shirt without a second thought—until I blurt, "That's my boob you're rubbing." He freezes. His face goes crimson.

"Shit—I'm so sorry. I wasn't thinking."

I smirk. Despite the ridiculousness of the situation, I'm… not mad. Somehow.

Now I'm standing in front of the hottest guy I've ever seen, with literal bird crap on my shoulder and coffee running down my shirt.

And to make matters worse, it's a white shirt. So now we're both looking at the black bra clearly visible underneath.

I clear my throat, trying to draw his eyes back up.

"I'm Patrick. Patrick Lawson," he says quickly. "Please let me buy you a new shirt—and a coffee. One you actually get to drink."

I laugh. It's involuntary. The first real laugh I've had in months.

"The coffee was yours, not mine."

He grins. And damn it—my heart actually skips.

He gestures toward the boutique across the street and pulls out his wallet.

"Please," he says, pressing a few folded notes into my hand.

"Let me at least fix the coffee part of this disaster."

I blink at the money, stunned. "Are you always this prepared for emergencies involving bird shit and public boob exposure?"

A grin tugs at the corner of his mouth. "It never hurts to be prepared."

Despite myself, I laugh. It's the first time something feels lighter in weeks.

I cross the street and head into the boutique. The sales assistant eyes the mess on my shirt with a mix of horror and sympathy, guiding me to the changing room with a blouse that doesn't scream "trauma victim." I change quickly, freshen up in the mirror, and step back outside.

Patrick is leaning against a lamppost, sunglasses on, casual and ridiculously attractive—like he belongs in a cologne advertisement. When he sees me, he straightens.

"Well," he says, scanning me from head to toe with a playful smirk, "if you were aiming to look even better than before… mission accomplished."

I feel heat rise to my cheeks. "You trying to make up for burning me?"

"Just evening the score," he says with a wink. "Come on. I still owe you a coffee. One that stays in the cup."

We head down the street to a cafe. Patrick holds the door open like a gentleman, and when I step inside, I swear something shifts in the air, like I've crossed some invisible line between ordinary and something else entirely.

I can't believe I've never been in this cafe before—it's cute, not overly busy. It has just the right amount of elegance and simplicity blended together. Soft jazz hums in the background, and tiny potted plants line the windowsills. The kind of place you'd want to write poetry in—or fall in love.

He pulls my chair out and then takes a seat across from me. "So gorgeous, are you going to tell me your name and why you looked a million miles from the world, when my coffee landed on you?"

"Lucy," I say simply. "Thanks for the shirt, Patrick."

He keeps asking questions—light ones at first—but soon, I can't help but spill more. It's like the words have been waiting to be heard.

"Both my parents were neurosurgeons," I tell him quietly. "They died in a car accident. A drunk driver. April 10th. Lookout Road."

His expression changes instantly. He stiffens. "What's wrong?" I ask, wary.

He hesitates. Then:

"That's the same night my dad died. He was the drunk driver."

The air leaves my lungs.

I stare at him.

Patrick's dad… killed my parents.

He pulls his hand away.

"I'm so sorry," he says. "I understand if you want me to leave."

But I don't let go of his hand.

"No. Please stay. I have questions."

We talk. He tells me about losing his mum to cancer, about his dad spiraling. It was the ten-year anniversary of her death that night.

He says, "I think he just couldn't carry the pain anymore. But it doesn't excuse what he did."

I don't know why, but I believe him. And I don't hate him.

Hours pass. We eat. We talk like we've known each other for years.

As we step out of the cafe, the sun has dipped lower in the sky, casting a soft golden glow across the pavement. People rush past, clinking shopping bags and chatting loudly. Everything feels louder than it did this morning. Or maybe… I'm just more awake.

We pause on the sidewalk. For a second, I don't want to say goodbye.

"I know today was a lot," Patrick says quietly. I nod. "Yeah. It was."

"But I'm glad I spilled coffee on you."

I laugh, despite everything. "Me too."

He shifts his weight slightly, then glances down with a small, almost shy smile.

"Can I have your phone?" he asks, voice low but warm.

I hesitate for half a second—old habits—but something in his eyes tells me I can trust him. I hand it over. He types in his number, saving it under **Patrick (Coffee Disaster)** with a teasing smirk, then sends himself a quick message so he has mine too.

"There," he says, handing it back. "Now if any more birds attack, you'll know who to call."

I laugh, but it catches in my throat when his hand lingers. His fingers gently brush over mine, deliberate and soft, like he's memorising the feel of my skin. The world feels quiet again, but not empty—full of something new. Something heavy and light all at once.

Then, slowly, he leans in.

His lips press against my forehead in a kiss that's more than friendly—but not quite romantic. Not yet. It's gentle. Reassuring. A promise without words.

"I'll call you," he whispers, so close I can feel the warmth of him.

My heart skips again.

And I really, really hope he does.

Chapter 3

Unfolding Truths

When I arrive home, a whirlwind of emotions crash over me. Heart pounding, hands trembling, and no matter how many deep breaths I take, I can't calm the storm inside me.

Feeling absolutely exhausted—but too wired to sleep.

Part of me wants to call Patrick.

But doesn't.

I call Sienna instead.

It rings twice before she picks up, out of breath. "Please tell me you're not dead in a ditch."

"I'm fine," I say, flopping onto the bed. "You're not going to believe, what just happened."

"Judging by your voice, I'd say either someone hot just kissed you, or hit you with their car."

"Closer to the second one, honestly."

And then I tell her. About the bird. The coffee. The white shirt and the very visible black bra. About Patrick's face when I snapped, "That's my boob you're rubbing." I tell her about the boutique, the new shirt, and the coffee we actually got to drink.

I leave out the part about who his dad is—at least for now. There's a long pause on her end.

"Well, shit," Sienna says finally. "That's either a terrible day or the start of a very sexy novel."

"Maybe both," I admit.

She hums. "Okay, but like… is he hot?"

I grin, even though she can't see it. "Stupid hot." "Well, damn. The grief goblin has taste."

I laugh, and for the first time in a long time, it's real. Full.

"You going to see him again?"

"I don't know. He said he'd call." Another pause.

"Lucy…"

"I know," I say quietly, reading her mind. "It's too soon. But it didn't feel wrong. It felt like… air."

Sienna doesn't argue.

She just says, "I'm here. Call me if he turns out to be a serial killer."

"I will."

Sienna hangs up first, but I don't move.

The silence feels louder now that the call is over. No background chatter. No banter. Just the quiet creak of the floorboards and the echo of my heartbeat.

I glance at my phone again. Still no message from Patrick. A part of me wants to reach out first.

The other part—the one still stitched together with fear and grief—refuses to break that silence.

To distract myself, I do the one thing I've been avoiding.

I walk down the hall and open Dad's office door.

The room has been untouched since the funeral. As I step in, I breathe in the familiar scent—wood polish and the faint trace of his aftershave. My chest tightens.

I sink into the leather chair at his desk and power on his computer. It takes three tries to guess the password. On the third—**Family**—the screen flickers to life.

A photo appears

It's the three of us on our last holiday to New Zealand—Dad with his arm around me, Mum mid-laugh, me beaming like life was perfect.

The image hits like a freight train.

There will never be another family holiday.

No more Christmas mornings in matching pyjamas. No more late-night chats when I couldn't sleep.

No more Dad.

I wipe my eyes and click into a folder labelled with his initials. I scroll through files until one catches my attention:

Referral: T. Lawson.

My pulse quickens.

I open it. It's a scanned letter addressed to my dad from a GP named Dr. Hargreaves.

Dear Dr. Mitchell,

I am referring Mr. Thomas Lawson, a 55-year-old male, for a neurological review following concerns involving short-term memory loss, erratic mood changes, and episodes of disorientation. Patient denies alcohol dependency but reports occasional use. Symptoms have worsened over the past two months. Please advise.

Sincerely, Dr. Andrew Hargreaves

I stare at the name.

Thomas Lawson.

Patrick's last name.

I checked the document's metadata—the referral was received just two weeks before the crash.

A chill creeps up my spine.

I sit there for what feels like hours, staring at the screen. What do I even do with this information? My dad tried to help Patrick's dad—and it still ended like this.

I feel sick. Like I've swallowed too much truth and now it's burning in my throat.

Was Patrick's dad sick? Was that what caused the crash? Or did no one listen in time?

This wasn't just a tragic coincidence. Our families were connected before the accident. And now, that truth might change everything.

I shut the laptop. My stomach twists as fresh grief mixes with a new fear.

Could I really let Patrick in, knowing this?

He was the first person to make me feel again. But what if everything between us is built on a secret that could destroy him?

I decided to call Sienna.

"I need to tell you something. It's about Patrick." "What? Did he say something weird?"

"His dad… his dad was the one driving the car. The one that hit my parents."

"Wait—what? Are you serious?"

"Dead serious. He told me before I found the letter. And now I found proof that my dad was supposed to see him, like, medically. It's all connected."

"Lucy. This is insane. You cannot seriously still be seeing this guy."

"I don't know what I'm doing. But I don't hate him."

"You don't have to hate him. But you also don't have to fall into him. Protect yourself, babe. Please."

I sit in the dark office for what feels like hours. The glow of the screen fades, but the name Thomas Lawson echoes in my mind like a warning I hadn't understood—until now.

Eventually, I crawl into bed. Like the night before, my eyes lock on the glowing digits of the clock.

Will he call me?

Would that be good… or a mistake?

And if he does…

Do I tell him what I found?

The same questions swirl, looping endlessly like a broken record. But eventually, my eyes grow heavy. Exhaustion pulls me under.

Beep. Beep. Beep.

I'm pulled from my sleep.

Groaning, I roll over and squint at the phone on my nightstand. My fingers hover just above it… then retreat.

What if it's Patrick?

What would I even say?

I haven't figured out how I feel, let alone what to do next. But curiosity wins. I grab my phone and rub my eyes, blinking at the screen.

Then, blinking again.

A message lights up my screen: *"Hey gorgeous, want to meet up today?"*

A small smile tugs at my lips. My cheeks flush with warmth.

It was the first time I'd smiled in months.

A tiny message… but a moment I'd never forget.

I don't know if it's because he called me gorgeous… or because I genuinely like this guy.

My fingers move before my brain catches up.

"sure"

One word.

That's all?

Brilliant, Lucy. Real smooth. Panic flickers in my chest.

Should I have said more?

But before I can overthink it, my phone **buzzes** again. *"Meet me at 11:30 under the oak tree by the lake."* Without hesitation, I type:

"okay"

Another one-word answer.

Classic.

I glance at the time—10:00 a.m.

Shit. I overslept.

Throwing off the covers, I bolt out of bed. Determined not to repeat yesterday's chaos (bird poop and boob coffee), I shower, straighten my hair, and even put on makeup for the first time in weeks.

I hesitate before leaving the house. My hand rests on the front doorknob, unsure if I'm ready for what today might bring. I press my forehead against the wood, eyes shut.

"You wanted this," I whisper to myself. And I did.

But part of me also wishes I could stay in the comfort of the unknown a little longer.

By 11:00, I'm out the door—nervous, excited, anxious like it's a first date.
I get to the lake five minutes early—didn't want to be late. Patrick's already there, leaning casually against the massive oak tree like he stepped out of a ROM-com.
When our eyes meet, my heart thuds. The wind whips my freshly straightened hair into disarray, but I barely notice.
As I near, I fumble—Do I hug him? Shake hands? Luckily, he makes the first move.

He steps forward and wraps me in a warm hug.

Well, hell, I think. Who am I to say no to hugging a hot guy?

When he pulls back, he gently tucks a strand of hair behind my ear.
"Hey, gorgeous," he says softly.
My heart lurches again.
Can he hear it? Can he see how fast it's racing?

I grab a hair tie from my wrist and throw my hair into a messy bun, hoping to quiet my nerves.

We begin walking around the lake. At first, there's silence. Not uncomfortable… but not quite easy either.

The gravel crunches under our feet as we circle the lake. The air smells like eucalyptus and fresh-cut grass. Kids' laughter echoes from the nearby playground, but it feels far away, like we're in a different bubble of time.

Finally, Patrick speaks. "How'd you sleep last night?"

This could've been it. My opening. The moment to tell him what I found.

Instead, I panic. "Good," I say.

One word.

Again.

Patrick chuckles gently. "You're not very chatty today, huh? Something on your mind?"

Another chance. Another opportunity to tell the truth. I hesitate. He sees it. He stops walking and takes my hand, warm, steady. "Lucy," he says, "you can tell me anything."

I look up at him. His eyes are soft, open, and full of something that makes me want to trust him.

"I'm not sure if you want to know this," I begin, barely whispering. "I don't even understand it myself—"

My phone rings. Loud and sudden. I check the screen—my

parents' lawyer.

"He doesn't wait for pleasantries. Just launches into talk of estate documents.

"Sorry," I mutter, stepping away. "It's my parents' lawyer. I have to take this."

The voice on the other end wasn't taking a breath between sentences. All I heard was Estate documents. Property transfer. Signing appointment.

I nod and respond mechanically, but my mind is still with Patrick.

When I hang up and return, his brow is furrowed.

"Everything okay?"

"Yeah, I think so. Just… legal stuff." He nods, then meets my eyes.

"I still want to know what you were going to tell me. No matter what it is."

He pauses.

"Meet me tonight? Same place we had lunch yesterday?" I hesitate. Then nod.

"Okay. I'll be there at seven."

As I walk toward my little red car, the same question plays in my head:

What will Patrick say when I tell him what I found?

Will he be angry? Hurt? Will he blame me?

But my thoughts keep drifting back to his voice, his touch, the way his fingers brushed mine like it wasn't the first time.

Stop it, Lucy. Focus.

You need to drive.

I grip the steering wheel, but my heart keeps racing—not from the road, but from Patrick.

And deep down, I know…

This was another moment I'd never forget.

That afternoon, when I pulled into the driveway and shut off the engine. The silence inside the car is almost deafening.

I reach for my phone and message Sienna.

"Just saw him again. Told him I had something to say…

Didn't say it, I was interrupted by a call from my parents' lawyers."

"Well, that was bad timing, what happened?"

"He asked me to meet him tonight. Said he wants to hear it." " I'm scared. What if it changes everything?"

"Then it does. But maybe it changes it in the right way." "Tell him. Be honest. That's all you can do."

"I've got wine on standby if it goes badly—and snacks if it goes well."

"Thanks. You always know what I need."

"You've got this, love you."

"Always."

As I set the phone down, exhale slowly, and head inside.

Tonight, everything might change. But at least I won't face it alone.

Chapter 4
The Truth Between Us

I've changed my outfit three times, reapplied my lip gloss twice, and spent the last fifteen minutes just staring at myself in the mirror, wondering if dinner tonight is a good idea.

Maybe this is stupid. Maybe it's brave. Maybe it's both.

What if this is the moment that changes everything? I can't stand him up. I have to tell him the truth.

My phone **buzzes.**

Sienna.

"You better send me a pic before you walk out that door."

I roll my eyes, but I do it.

Snap. Mirror selfie. Hair curled, dress snug in all the right places, nerves showing just slightly in my eyes.

I send it with a caption: *"Be honest. Too much?"*

Her reply is instant: *"Too much?? You look HOT. Like, 'I know my ex is still stalking my Instagram' hot. Like funeral-chic goddess levels of hot." "Is that... a thing?"*

"It is now. Damn, Luce. If this guy doesn't fall at your feet, he's an idiot."

I pause, fingers hovering over the screen, then type:

"Patrick."

Three dots appear. Then stop. Then appear again.

"Still Patrick?" "Still." "Lucy…"

I exhale, already knowing what's coming. "I know what you're going to say."

"Then I'll say it anyway. I get that you feel something. I get that he's hot. But his dad killed your parents. That's not just baggage— that's a shipping container full of trauma."

"You think I don't know that?"

"I think you do, but I also think you're lonely. And vulnerable. And maybe hoping that if something good can come from something awful, then it makes the awful a little less awful."

I stare at the message. The ache in my chest says she's not wrong.

"I'm not looking for a fairy tale, Sienna."

"I know you're not. But you are looking for something to feel again. Just… promise me you're not walking into this because it's easier than walking through the grief."

I blink back a sudden sting of tears.

"He makes me feel like I can breathe."

Another pause. Then: *"Okay. But if he breaks you, I'm showing up with a shovel and a really good alibi."*

I smile through the burn in my throat.

"Love you."

"Always. Go knock him dead. Just emotionally. Not, like… actual murder. You've had enough of that."

"Dark."

"You picked me as your best friend. You knew what you were getting."

I swipe on lip gloss for the third time, grab my purse, and head out the door before I change my mind again.

As I drive to the restaurant, my thoughts drift—again. And this time, they go exactly where they shouldn't: straight to Patrick. More specifically, what he might look like under his clothes.

Does he have abs?

Does he have that sexy crease line that runs from his hips… down?

Ugh.

Lucy, stop it.

You cannot let your thoughts hijack your brain like this. Not tonight.

But of course, the more I try not to think about it, the clearer the image becomes.

Patrick's toned stomach. My fingers tracing every line of muscle, feeling the dip of that V-shaped line just above his waistband…

God.

Focus, woman. You are not thirteen with a celebrity crush. You're about to have a serious conversation with the guy whose dad killed your parents.

Still, I feel my cheeks flush as I grip the steering wheel tighter. This night is going to be complicated.

As I continue the drive, I catch glimpses of the familiar town passing by—the bakery Mum loved, the bookstore where Dad used to sneak in and buy me new releases before I even knew they'd launched. Everything feels the same. And yet, nothing is.

My hands tighten on the steering wheel. I wonder what they'd say if they knew I was going to dinner with the son of the man who ended their lives.

Maybe they'd understand. Maybe they'd tell me grief doesn't follow rules. That healing comes in strange, beautiful, messy forms.

I breathe in sharply.

Maybe this isn't betrayal. Maybe it's survival.

When I park and catch a glimpse of myself in the rearview mirror, I second-guess my choice to come tonight.

Actually, it's more like my third… maybe even fourth guess.

But still, I take a deep breath, step out of the car, and head toward the restaurant.

The second I step inside, I see him. Patrick.

He's already looking at me, and for a moment, the entire room fades away. It's just him. That smile. And the warmth it sends rushing through my chest.

God, I wonder if he's been mentally undressing me like I've been doing to him.

As I walk toward him, the room slowly comes back into focus. Patrick stands, pulls out my chair—such a gentleman.

I sit, nerves buzzing beneath my skin.

"I'm glad you came," he says, his voice low and sincere. "Honestly, I wasn't sure you would after earlier… we clearly left a lot unsaid."

I nod, forcing a small smile.

"Honestly? I wasn't sure if I was going to come. But I know you deserve the truth—or at least what little I know of it."

"You seem nervous," Patrick says gently, after the drinks arrive.

I laugh, too quickly. "Is it that obvious?"

"Only a little. But don't worry—I'm nervous too."

I glance up. "You? Nervous? You seem…completely put together."

He shrugs. "You're kind of a big deal, Lucy."

The words hit differently. There's no teasing. He means it.

Just as I'm about to tell him everything I found on my dad's computer, I hear a voice from behind me.

"Hi, Lucy." I freeze.

No… not now.

Of all the ghosts from my past, he had to be the one to crash into this moment.

Standing beside our table is Zeke.

Of all the times he could have shown up in the past couple of months, it had to be now, while I'm sitting opposite Patrick, about to bare my soul.

Zeke's eyes flick from me to Patrick. I can see he's waiting for some kind of introduction.

"Hi, Zeke," I say tightly. "This is Patrick. Patrick, this is… uh… Zeke. An old friend."

They both glance at me with the same unspoken look:

Yeah, right.

Zeke's voice softens. "How are you, Lucy? I've been meaning to reach out but… I wasn't sure if you'd want me to."

I want to scream. Not here. Not now.

"I'm okay. Taking it one day at a time," I reply, forcing politeness. "But I'm in the middle of something right now. I'll… message you later."

A lie. Obviously. But I need him gone.

Zeke nods. "No worries. Enjoy your night." And just like that, he walks away.

Before I can even turn back, Patrick speaks.

"So," he says, raising an eyebrow, "are you going to tell me who that really was? Because there was enough tension between you two to power the entire room."

I don't know which conversation would be worse— Telling Patrick what I found on Dad's computer…

Or telling him how I really knew Zeke. Patrick sees the worry creeping into my face.

He leans forward slightly, voice calm and even. "I'm guessing he's your ex?"

I hesitate.

Do I lie? Keep it vague?

But before I can decide, my mouth answers for me.

"We were dating," I blurt. "Back then. The night my parents died, actually. I stayed home because I wanted to spend time with him. I thought we might… take the next step. But I changed my mind at the last minute."

I can't bring myself to look at Patrick.

"I didn't go with them because of him. Because I was being selfish. And ever since that night, I keep wondering—if I'd just gone with them, maybe none of this would've happened."

There. It's out. Almost all of it. When I finally look up, Patrick just stares at me. Not angry. Not shocked. Just… quiet.

"I didn't know how to tell you," I add softly. "Because I already feel like I carry part of the blame. And I wasn't sure if, after everything, you'd still look at me the same."

Then he says the one thing I wasn't expecting.

"So… did you stop things with Zeke that night because you're a virgin and you weren't ready? Or because you didn't want him to be your first?"

My eyes widen as heat rushes to my cheeks. I blink at him, stunned.

He raises both hands quickly.

"Sorry! I didn't mean to make you blush."

"No, it's not that. I just… wasn't expecting that to be your first question after everything I said."

He laughs, soft and easy. It eases something tight in my chest. "But to answer your question…" I pause, taking a breath.

"Yes. I'm a virgin. And I'm not sure why I stopped that night—it just didn't feel right. But looking back now, I know for sure… Zeke isn't the guy I want my first time to be with."

There. Honest. No filter. And for once, I don't regret it. Patrick leans in slightly, eyes locked on mine.

"I'm glad you stopped… because if, when the time is right, it should be with someone who makes you feel safe. Someone who makes you feel… everything."

The waitress appears, notebook in hand, bright smile on her

face.

"Hi, I'm Georgia, and I'll be your waitress again. What can I get you both tonight?"

We both chuckle—clearly she remembers us from yesterday. Patrick orders a steak, medium rare.

I go with the salmon.

As Georgia walks away, Patrick turns back to me.

"You know," he says gently, "the accident would've happened whether or not you were in that car. The only difference is… you wouldn't be here. And I wouldn't be sitting here with the most gorgeous girl I've ever met."

Before I can respond, he takes my hand across the table.

"And now," he continues, "I think it's time you told me what you were going to say earlier today."

I swallow hard.

He senses my hesitation and squeezes gently.

"Lucy," he says softly, "nothing you say will change the way I feel about you. Or what's happening between us."

His words calm the storm just enough to find my voice.

"When I got home yesterday," I begin slowly, "I went through Dad's office. I didn't get very far, but I opened a folder I didn't recognise. And I found something."

Patrick listens, silent and steady.

"There was a name that stood out… Thomas Lawson." Patrick's jaw tightens, just slightly.

"That's my dad's name," he says, brows drawing together.

I nod. "Yeah. It was a referral letter—from a local GP—sent to my dad. Your dad was being referred for a neurological evaluation."

Patrick blinks. "For what?"

"The letter mentioned memory lapses, mood swings, disorientation… and that alcohol made it worse. The referral was dated two weeks before the accident."

His expression shifts—quiet shock.

"There was a note from my dad, too. He hadn't seen your dad yet, but he was reviewing the file. He thought it could be something serious… maybe frontal lobe trauma. He said alcohol would only intensify it."

Patrick exhales slowly.

"So you're saying… he might not have just been drunk that night."

"No," I say softly. "Something else might've been wrong. And the alcohol… just made it worse."

He leans back in his seat, letting it sink in.

"So your dad was going to help him?" he asks.

"Maybe," I whisper. "But he never got the chance."

We sit in silence as our food arrives. Neither of us touches it at first.

When we finally eat,   it's slow and thoughtful. Neither of us was rushing to fill the silence.

Then Patrick looks at me again. His voice is quiet but sure. "This doesn't change how I feel about you."

Before I can say anything, I blurt out, "It doesn't change how I feel either."

He smiles and stands to walk me to my car.

We stroll in silence beneath the night sky. When we reach my car, he leans close.

His voice is low and warm against my ear.

"Can I kiss you?"

"Yes."

No hesitation.

He tucks a strand of hair behind my ear and cups my face gently. His breath is soft against my cheek, then his lips meet mine.

Our first kiss.

Soft. Sure. Sweet. Slow. Unbelievably warm.

We kiss like we've been waiting for it for years—without ever knowing it.

When he pulls back, I already miss him. He smiles.

"Goodnight, gorgeous."

"Goodnight, Patrick," I whisper, still tasting him.

As I watch him walk away, hands in pockets, shoulders relaxed in the moonlight, I touch my lips with my fingers.

That kiss wasn't just a kiss.

It was a release. A start. A moment I know I'll replay for years.

I open the car door, sit behind the wheel, and let the silence wrap around me like a blanket.

Then, without overthinking it, I pull out my phone and send a message to Sienna:

"He kissed me. I think I'm screwed."

Chapter 5

Uninvited

The porch light glows softly as I turn onto the long, sweeping driveway, flanked by manicured hedges and towering trees lit by subtle ground lights. The tires crunch over the smooth stone path, winding toward the grand front entrance. The house— more like an estate—rises ahead, stately and serene, with soft amber lights glowing from the wide front windows. My heart still flutters from Patrick's kiss. His touch lingers on my skin, warm and electric, and every part of me feels… awake.

But as I step out of the car and glance up, I freeze.

Someone's sitting on the front steps—legs stretched out casually, one arm draped over the railing like they've been waiting a while. The porch light casts a soft glow over them, outlining a familiar silhouette in the fading dusk

Zeke.

He stands when he sees me, brushing his hands on his jeans like he doesn't know what to do with them.

"Hey," he says quietly.

"What are you doing here?" I ask, surprised but not entirely shocked.

He shrugs. "Just… wanted to check in. I hadn't heard from you."

"I told you I'd message you later."

"Yeah, I guess I just…" He trails off, eyes flicking down my dress. "Didn't expect you to be out. Like that. Dressed like that."

I fold my arms. "Like what?"

He hesitates, then says it anyway. "Dressed up. On a date." My chest tightens. "I never said it was a date."

"You didn't have to." His tone isn't angry—it's hurt. "I saw you. With him."

I say nothing.

Zeke's jaw clenches. "So that's it? You're just… moving on?"

"I'm not moving on, Zeke," I say, trying to keep my voice even. "I'm surviving. One breath at a time."

He shakes his head. "I just don't get it. A few weeks ago, you could barely leave   the   house.   And   now   you're… smiling. Laughing. With some guy I've never even seen before."

"That 'some guy' is kind. He listens. He doesn't tiptoe around me like I'm broken."

Zeke winces. "I never thought you were broken." "You treat

me like I might shatter any second." "I was trying to give you space!"

"Well, maybe I needed someone who wasn't afraid to be there."

We both fall quiet. The silence feels heavier than anything we've said.

Then he asks, softer, "Are you sleeping with him?" I blink. "Wow."

"I just need to know where I stand, Lucy."

"You don't," I say simply. "Because we're not together." His face twists slightly, like I just punched him. "Right."

He turns to go, pausing at the bottom of the steps.

"I just miss you," he says, not looking back.

"You obviously didn't miss me enough to turn up when I needed you the most and for that I will never forgive you."

"You won't there the morning of the funeral when I was still in my pyjamas. Still numb. Still curled up on the bathroom floor.

You didn't come to help me get dressed.

You never called or checked in.

Didn't ask if I needed anything.

You showed up to the funeral, sure—standing stiff in the third row, eyes on the ground like you were attending a stranger's service.

No hug. No words. No "I'm here for you."

Just a silent figure in a sea of black… and then nothing. No message. No visit. No checking in after everyone else left.

And now your here—on my front steps—asking if I'm sleeping with someone else?"

Zeke has no response, no I'm sorry, no nothing. He just nods his head walks away.

I wait until I can't see him anymore, then head inside and close the door behind me.

The silence that follows is louder than his footsteps.

I lock the door behind me and lean into it. Exhaling hard, heart still racing. Not from Patrick this time… but from the ghost I thought I'd left on the steps of my past.

I head to my bedroom, slip out of the dress, and grab my phone from the nightstand.

A new message from Sienna lights up the screen:

"OMG, he kissed you! Was there fireworks? Details, woman."

I stare at it for a beat before typing:

"Yes. It was perfect. But guess who was sitting on my front steps when I got home?"

Three dots.

"Zeke."

"You're kidding."

"I wish."

"What did he say?"

"That he missed me. That he didn't expect me to be out. Dressed up. On a date."

"Let me guess—he looked wounded and broody and a little too handsome for his own good?"

"Exactly."

"Ugh. Typical ex-energy. Silent until you smile again."

"He asked if I was sleeping with Patrick."

"WHAT?"

"Yeah."

"I swear, if he keeps pulling this wounded-puppy crap, I'm going to throw a casserole dish at his head."

"Please don't. I like those dishes."

"Fine. But if he shows up again uninvited, I'm coming over.

With wine. And emotional support slaps."

I smile—tired, but grateful.

"Thanks, love you."

"Always. Now go to bed, and get your beauty rest."

Just as I go to place my phone on the nightstand, it **buzzes**. One word:

"More."

One word. Loaded. Dangerous. And impossible to ignore

My heart skips. My skin prickles at the word. One syllable, and I'm melting.

I type back instantly:

"When and where?"

I didn't know what would happen next—but I already knew: This was becoming something I'd never forget.

Chapter 6

Dinner, Dancing, and Secrets

As I fall asleep, for the first time in a long time, I feel happy. Peaceful. My body relaxes into the mattress, and my mind drifts away, lost in thoughts of Patrick—anything and everything Patrick.

The morning rays peek through my curtains, warm and gentle. The birds are chirping, and the house is quiet. Comfortably quiet.

I roll over and reach for my phone. One new message lights up the screen:

"Morning, Gorgeous. Today, 6 p.m. Your place."

My smile widens, and I don't even hesitate. I sent him my address immediately.

I crawl out of bed, stretching, as I make my way to the kitchen, I realise… "Oh shit."

The house is a mess. Like, full-blown tornado-hit-it mess. Cleaning hasn't exactly been high on my list of priorities lately.

Well, it is now.

I throw my hair into a messy bun, crank up the music, and get to work. Dishes first, then the lounge room. Before I know it, I'm dancing with a mop in hand, lip-syncing into a wooden spoon like it's a microphone. It feels ridiculous—and freeing.

The Moments I'll Never Forget

It's the first time in months I've felt light. Alive.

Is it because of Patrick? Or is it just the first glimmer of healing? Maybe both.

But my moment of musical bliss is interrupted when I glance at the clock.

5:00 p.m.

Cue panic.

The house looks amazing, but I look like a human disaster. I bolt upstairs and jump into the shower, scrubbing quickly while mentally debating what the hell to wear.

I don't know what Patrick has planned, but I want to feel confident.

I pull out the little black dress I wore to my eighteenth birthday party—the one that hugs my curves in all the right places. It still fits like a dream.

Feeling brave, I reach for a bold red lipstick instead of my usual soft gloss. I swipe it on, then pause, puckering at the mirror. It's daring—too daring?

I hover over the makeup wipes, second-guessing myself. And then—**Ding Dong**.

The doorbell rings.

My heart jumps. It has to be Patrick.

I take a deep breath and begin walking—no, gliding—down the stairs. He can see me through the glass panels, and I want to look like I've got my life together. Cool. Confident. Sexy in slow motion.

Not like someone who's one misstep away from tumbling ass over head down the stairs in a heap of red lipstick and nerves.

I open the door to find Patrick standing there, a bunch of flowers in his hand.

"Natives? For me?" I ask, genuinely surprised. "Wow, thanks! How did you know they were my favourite?"

He chuckles. "I didn't. The florist told me they'd last longer than all the others."

His honesty makes me laugh. "That's… actually a pretty solid reason."

I step aside and push the door open wider, letting him in.

Patrick walks in, taking in the space. His eyes go straight to the staircase. "Wow. That's big."

Without thinking, I blurt, "I hope that's not the only thing that's big."

Oh. My. God.

I freeze. Eyes wide. Did those words just come out of my mouth?!

"Shit," I mutter under my breath, my face already burning. "That was supposed to stay in my head."

Patrick turns to me, eyebrows raised, clearly amused. We lock eyes. I have no idea what to say to make this less awkward.

But then, without missing a beat, his gaze drifts slowly down my body… then back up again, a little smirk tugging at his lips.

"You look stunning tonight, gorgeous," he says softly. "Absolutely stunning."

My breath catches. Just like that, the awkwardness melts into something warmer… heavier. His voice. That look in his eyes.

I might've embarrassed myself two minutes ago, but judging by the way he's looking at me now… I think he liked it.

"Where's the kitchen, Lucy?"

I point toward it. "Follow me."

As we walk, neither of us says a word, but I can feel his eyes on me the entire time. Heat rises to my cheeks—and other places.

When we reach the kitchen, he pauses and looks at me with a grin. "Can I follow you back to the front door?"

I blink. "Why?"

He smirks, completely unbothered. "Because I like watching your ass when you walk in front of me."

My jaw drops. My cheeks turn crimson in half a second.

Before I can say anything, he steps forward and places his hands on my hips. This time, he doesn't ask. He just leans in and kisses me.

And holy hell—I'm pretty sure fireworks are going off around us.

His lips are even softer than before, his tongue sliding into my mouth with such slow, perfect confidence that I melt into him.

Then, right as his hands move from my hips to cup my ass…

RRRRRRGGGGGGGHHHHH.

My stomach lets out a growl so loud it sounds like a bear just walked into the kitchen.

Patrick pulls back, his hands still firmly on my backside, and grins. "Sounds like you're hungry."

I try to downplay it. "No, I'm good." Lies. Massive lies.

I'd been so caught up cleaning the house that I forgot to eat all day. But right now, the last thing I want to do is stop kissing him. Well, maybe not the last thing…

"I brought ingredients for us to cook dinner," he says.

"Cook?"

"Yes. We're going to cook dinner together."

I snort. "I've barely cooked in my life. I've never needed to. The delivery guy and I are basically on a first-name basis."

Patrick laughs. "Well, tonight you're learning how to cook spaghetti. It's not hard, I promise."

He says the word hard and all I can think about is what was

pressed up against me a minute ago…

God, focus, Lucy.

He opens the bag of groceries and glances around. "Where do you keep the pots and pans?"

I shrug. "One of those cupboards, I guess."

He starts opening doors, one by one, until he finally finds them.

I stand at the counter, chopping whatever ingredients he places in front of me while he does pretty much everything else. The smell of garlic and tomatoes starts filling the air, and steam rises from the stovetop.

I lean over his shoulder and smirk. "It's getting hot in here." He smirks back without missing a beat. "Yeah, it is."

And yeah… it is. But I'm not sure how much the boiling water has to do with it.

As dinner finishes cooking, I grab two bowls from the cupboard.

"At least you know where the bowls are," he teases with a laugh.

We sit at the table, spaghetti steaming in front of us, and just… talk.

Simple questions at first.

"What's your favourite colour?" he asks.

"Pink. Yours?"
"Blue."

"What's your favourite food?"

"For the last two months? Anything I could get delivered to my door. But now…" I smile, twirling my fork. "Spaghetti."
He grins. "Anything Italian."

The questions go back and forth—fun, lighthearted things that help us peel back each other's layers. I can feel myself relaxing, laughing more freely than I have in a long time.
Then there's a pause in the conversation.

And I realise—I want to know something. A question I've never asked anyone before, but it's been echoing in my head all night.
So I take a breath. "Can I ask you something kind of personal?"
He nods. "Sure."

"How many girls have you had sex with?"

His eyes lock onto mine, and I can tell I've caught him off guard. Not in a bad way—just… surprised.
He doesn't answer right away. And I wonder if he's trying

to figure out what number won't scare me off.

But finally, he exhales. "I took a minute to answer because I didn't want you to think less of me… but the truth is—I've never had sex before."

I stare at him. I know the shock on my face must be obvious, because he continues, almost nervously.

"When my mum died, I was in a really bad place. I acted out a lot and made life hell for my dad. Even though I was twelve, I was a real shithead. By the time I turned sixteen, I was sick of it—sick of myself, honestly.

One day, I went to visit my mum's grave… something I'd never done before. Sitting there, talking to her, I realised she'd be ashamed of how I'd been living."

He pauses, and I say nothing—just listen.

"After that, I decided to pull my shit together. I started actually trying at school. And because I was already so far behind, I had to work twice as hard to catch up. I didn't know what I wanted to do after school, but I was good at maths, so I went into accounting. I finished my degree last year."

Another pause, softer this time.

"There just wasn't really time for girls. Don't get me wrong— there's been a few kisses here and there, but nothing serious. Nothing worth chasing. Until now."

His eyes find mine again.

And suddenly, I don't care about the number. I don't care that it's zero. In fact, I love that it's zero. Because it's real. Honest. Brave.

And it makes me like him even more.

Patrick leans back in his chair slightly, his gaze warm but curious.

"Since we're diving into personal stuff now…" he starts, his voice a little hesitant, "I know you said you're a virgin, but can I ask why?"

I blink, surprised—but not offended.

"You're gorgeous," he adds quickly. "I mean, guys must've been throwing themselves at you for years. And I know you've had at least one boyfriend…" He gives a half-smile. "Remember our awkward encounter with Zeke?"

That makes me laugh softly.

"And speaking of Zeke… did you ever text him like you said you would?"

Wow. That was a lot.

I sit there for a second, letting the weight of his honesty— and now his curiosity—settle around me. He was open with me. It's only fair that I do the same.

I take a breath. "Yeah, there've been guys interested in me. But none that I was really interested in back."

He listens quietly, his eyes never leaving mine.

"Zeke and I… we dated for a while. But we were friends first, and I think that's why I said yes when he asked me out. It felt safe. Familiar. Comfortable."

I pause for a moment, choosing my next words carefully.

"And yeah, we made out a bit—okay, a lot," I admit, laughing a little. "But when it came to going further, I just… couldn't. There was no chemistry. No spark. No butterflies."

I glance up at Patrick, my cheeks heating. "Definitely no fireworks. Not like the ones I get when you kiss me."

The second the words leave my mouth, I want to crawl under the table.

"Oh my God," I mutter. "I wasn't supposed to say that part out loud."

Patrick laughs, a full, warm sound that fills the room. He leans closer, eyes locked on mine.

"Fireworks, huh?" he says, a grin tugging at the corner of his mouth. "Glad I'm not the only one feeling them."

I smile, biting my lip.

"And to answer your last question… no, I never texted

Zeke."

"The only guy I've texted since I met you…" I say, reaching out and gently brushing my fingers against his, "is you. And the only guy I want to keep texting is you."

Well, technically I'm not lying—I didn't text Zeke.

Patrick twirls spaghetti around his fork and glances up at me and nods, like he's relieved.

And I let the conversation move on, even though my mind lingers in that shadowed space between honesty and omission.

Chapter 7

A Night To Remember

Now that the last question has been asked, our bowls are empty, and my stomach can no longer betray me with dramatic growls, we decide to clean up.

Patrick washes while I dry—an easy rhythm between us. "This feels familiar," I say softly, glancing at him.

He looks over, curious. "Why?"

"It's exactly what my parents used to do after dinner. Dad washed, Mum dried."

A lump rises in my throat, and before I can stop it, a tear slips down my cheek. Patrick notices instantly. He gently takes the towel from my hands, wipes his hands dry, and then—so tenderly—brushes the tear from my face.

His touch is soft. Comforting.

"It's okay," I whisper. "I know there will always be moments in life that remind me of them. And yeah, sometimes they'll hurt… but honestly, I think that's a good thing. It means I'll always carry them with me. Their love for each other. And for me."

Patrick gives me a quiet smile, understanding without saying a word.

Then he lifts the towel again, a playful glint flashing in his eyes.

"Wanna see something I remember my mum and Dad doing?"

I nod, genuinely curious. "Of course."

He waves the towel. "Run."

My eyebrows shoot up. "What?"

"Run!" he says again, grinning now.

And something in me—something light and mischievous I haven't felt in years—makes me do exactly that.

I bolt.

I can hear his laughter behind me as he chases me through the house, brandishing the towel like a weapon of joy. I look back over my shoulder just in time to see him close the distance.

God, he's gorgeous when he laughs.

And honestly? I want him to catch me.

I slow just enough, and—whack—the edge of the towel flicks against my butt.

"Ha! **Got ya!**" he laughs.

I spin around, breathless, flushed from the chase and something else entirely.

Patrick looks around, taking in the space around us. "Wow…

I didn't realise how big your house was."

"Yeah," I say, glancing at the high ceilings and wide halls. "Sometimes it feels even bigger than it is."

He steps closer, still slightly out of breath, eyes gleaming. "Wanna give me the grand tour?"

"Sure, follow me," I say, shooting him a playful look.

"Oh yeah, I like it when I get to follow you," he replies, that cheeky grin tugging at his lips.

I grin back and bite my bottom lip, teasing. "Well, you've seen most of the downstairs already, but we'll do a quick lap."

We walk through the main floor, Patrick trailing just close enough to keep his eyes locked on my body but far enough behind that I can feel his gaze lingering.

I point out each room one by one. "Kitchen, lounge room, laundry, guest bedroom and ensuite… and the main downstairs bathroom."

"What's upstairs?" he asks, eyes flicking toward the grand staircase.

We pause at the base of the stairs. I turn to him, smirking.

"You can lead the way this time. I'll follow. You won't get lost before making it to the top."

His brows raised in amusement. "Fair's fair—you've had your turn watching my ass. Now it's my turn."

He doesn't argue—just laughs, nods, and starts up the

staircase, step by slow step, very aware that I'm watching. And damn, the view is good.

Once we reach the top, he turns back. "Okay, now we're even."

We walk side by side again as I point out each room. Some he pokes his head into, taking quick peeks.

"Main bathroom. Guest rooms one, two and three. Home gym. Library—"

"You have a library?" he interrupts, clearly impressed.

"Yep," I say with a little shrug. "And a theatre room." I gesture toward it.

His jaw drops slightly as he looks in, clearly not used to this kind of space. I can see it on his face—his house definitely isn't like mine.

We keep walking.

The next door is shut. "What's in there?" he asks.

"That was my parents' room. I haven't opened that door since they passed."

He nods gently, understanding without needing me to explain more.

"Next is Dad's office," I say, pointing to another door. "And the one at the end of the hall… that's mine."

Patrick grins. "Well, aren't you going to show me your

room?" I hesitate.

In all the cleaning I did earlier today, I hadn't touched my room. It's a mess—clothes everywhere, an unmade bed, laundry I've been ignoring for a week.

"Ah… maybe next time. I didn't really get to clean it."

He shakes his head. "I don't care, Lucy. I want to get to know all of you. That includes your messy room."

With a sigh and a smile, I open the door.

He steps inside, not even noticing the mess. His eyes go straight to the window.

"Whoa. You have a pool."

"Yep. And a tennis court. Basketball court, too. And on the actual ground floor—below the main level—there's a bowling alley and an arcade room."

He turns to me, laughing like he thinks I'm joking. "The ground floor? We were just there."

"Nope," I reply with a smirk. "Technically, what we were on earlier is Level One. The actual ground floor—the basement level—is under that. There's a staircase next to the kitchen that leads down."

He stares at me for a beat, then realises I'm not kidding.

"Jesus, Lucy," he says, laughing again. "Are you secretly

royalty or something?"

"I know that was a rhetorical question," I say, smirking, "but I feel like it needs an answer. Not at all. But remember—both my parents were neurosurgeons. They made some great investments."

Patrick raises an eyebrow, clearly impressed.

"I really want to stay in here with you," he continues, glancing around my bedroom, "but the kid in me really wants to see that arcade room."

I grin. "Of course you do. Everyone always wants to see the arcade room."

We head back down the hallway. I pause beside a door. "Want to take the stairs or the lift?"

Patrick blinks. "Wait—you have a lift in your house?"

"Yep." I open the door, revealing a sleek private elevator. "Well? Your choice."

"Lift. Definitely the lift."

We step inside. The doors close behind us, and I press the button for the lower level. The elevator hums softly as it begins to descend, but Patrick doesn't take his eyes off me. His gaze lingers, warm and charged, like he's not sure if he wants to kiss me or pin me against the wall.

The tension between us is thick, humming in the air like static before a storm. My skin prickles under the weight of his attention. I lick my lips without thinking, and his jaw clenches just slightly.

When the doors slide open, I exhale the breath I didn't realise I was holding.

"Down here," I say, stepping out, "you'll find the bowling alley, the arcade, and my own mini nightclub."

Patrick's eyebrows shoot up. "Nightclub? You never mentioned that upstairs."

I shrug like it's no big deal. "Oh yeah, I guess I forgot. I haven't really used it much—just for my eighteenth birthday party."

"You literally have a nightclub in your house and forgot to mention it?" he laughs.

"What can I say? It slips my mind sometimes." I throw him a wink.

He looks around like a kid in the world's coolest candy store. "Where do we even start?"

I raise an eyebrow. "Bowling? Arcade? Dance floor?"

He doesn't hesitate. "Honestly, I love arcade games... but all I really want to do right now is watch you dance."

I roll my eyes playfully. "If I have to dance, you have to dance with me."

"Deal."

I walk over to the DJ controls—yes, my own private DJ

setup— and press a few buttons. Lights on the dance floor flicker to life beneath our feet, casting colourful glows around the room. Music pours out of the speakers—loud, bassy, and perfect.

And I couldn't have picked a better song if I tried.

Patrick watches me, eyes locked on mine, waiting for me to move.

So I do.

I start slowly, hips swaying, letting the rhythm pulse through me. The music fills the space, and the heat between us builds with every beat. He steps forward and joins me, hands finding my waist as we fall into sync without a word.

Our bodies move together like they've been doing this for years.

His hands slide around to the small of my back, pulling me a little closer.

And damn, if this isn't the hottest slow-burn build-up of my entire life.

We move together, hips swaying in sync, his body pressed so firmly against mine that I can feel everything—and I mean everything. His head, once resting so peacefully on my shoulder, slowly lifts. His eyes find mine, and for a moment, it's like he's looking straight into my soul.

One of his hands slides behind my head, fingers threading

through my hair. Just when I think our bodies couldn't possibly get any closer, his other hand grips my lower back and pulls me into him, hard. That subtle thrust sends a shiver through me, and before he can even make the first move, I kiss him.

He doesn't hesitate. Not even for a second.

This kiss is nothing like the others. It's hard, fast, hungry, desperate. I want to rip his clothes off right here on the dance floor, consequences be damned. But I know I shouldn't. Not yet.

When it becomes clear we've reached the edge—when this kiss can't escalate any further without setting the room on fire—we finally pull back, both breathless.

Patrick rests his forehead against mine, our breaths still tangled in the space between us.

"I could get lost in you," he murmurs, barely audible above the music.

My hands slide down to his chest, feeling the rapid beat of his heart beneath my palms.

"Maybe we both already are," I whisper.

His eyes are dark, chest heaving, and I know I look just as hot and flustered as he does.

"Lucy," he murmurs, "I want to fall asleep with you in my arms tonight. Just that. Nothing more. Just… to hold you while we sleep."

I take a moment to calm the storm inside me. My whole body is aching for more—but my heart? It's steady. It knows this is exactly what I need.

"That sounds perfect."

We turn off the lights downstairs and take the elevator back up, hand in hand, the silence between us warm and comfortable. At my bedroom door, Patrick pauses, then reaches for my hand again.

"I promise, Lucy," he says softly, "I'll control myself. Even though every part of me wants to rip your clothes off and ravish every inch of you… we have plenty of time for that. Tonight—we just sleep."

"Ripping my clothes off does sound fun," I tease, grinning, "but yeah… sleep is definitely needed tonight."

He climbs onto the bed and as he does, I stand there watching him get comfortable.

I pause at the edge of the bed, suddenly unsure.

What if I wake up from one of my nightmares? What if he sees the broken pieces I usually keep buried?

He notices the hesitation in my eyes. "You okay?"

I nod too quickly. "Yeah. Just… haven't shared a bed with anyone since… well. Ever."

His face softens. "Then we'll go slow. No pressure, Lucy.

Just sleep."

"Come on," he says, patting the bed. "I'll be the big spoon. You be the little spoon."

I smile and climb into bed, curling into his warmth. His arms wrap around me so perfectly, like they were made to hold me.

He presses a kiss to the back of my neck and whispers, "Goodnight, gorgeous."

All I can manage is a quiet, "Goodnight, Patrick," as I try to slow my breathing and quiet the flurry of thoughts inside my head.

He hums against my skin. "You smell like strawberries." I laugh. "That's probably just my shampoo."

"Still. I like it."

We fall quiet for a moment, the kind of silence that doesn't need to be filled.

"Thank you for tonight," I murmur. "For not pushing."

"You're not something to push, Lucy," he says. "You're someone to hold onto."

For so long, my bed had been a place of silence, grief, and sleepless nights. But tonight, it holds something else—hope. Safety. Him

His body stays pressed against mine, solid and safe, and before long, I drift off to sleep, wrapped in him.

And I already know… this is definitely a moment I'll never forget.

Chapter 8

The Pink Folder

As my body begins to stir, I feel the warmth of Patrick's breath on the back of my neck, his arm still wrapped tightly around me.

Then it hits me—oh crap. He's going to see my very not-so-attractive morning look.

I have to freshen up before he wakes. There's no way this version of me is going to be the first thing he sees when he opens his eyes.

Very carefully, I lift his arm and slide out of bed, creeping toward the bathroom without making a sound.

I splash water on my face, wiping away the smudged mascara under my eyes. I brush my teeth, banishing the dreaded morning breath, and run my fingers through my hair to smooth it down.

As I tiptoe out of the bathroom and head back toward the bed, Patrick begins to stir. I slip under the covers just in time for his eyes to flutter open and land on me.

"Wow," he says, voice still raspy with sleep. "You're even gorgeous first thing in the morning."

I laugh, knowing that wasn't the case two minutes earlier. "Did you have plans today?" he asks, stretching.

"Not really," I reply. "But I was thinking I might try to clear out my dad's office. I didn't get very far last time I tried."

Patrick looks at me thoughtfully, like he knows it's something I shouldn't be doing alone.

"Would you like some help?" he offers.

"Yeah, actually… I wouldn't mind that."

"Great. Mind if I use your shower first?"

"Not at all. There are fresh towels in the cupboard. I'll go make us some coffee."

I head downstairs while Patrick showers. But while trying to make coffee, all I can think about is him—Patrick in my shower, the hot steam, his naked body…

I stand there, totally spaced out, imagination in overdrive, when I hear a voice behind me.

"What happened to the coffee?"

Oh crap. I've been standing here daydreaming and didn't even get started.

"Umm… slight distraction," I say, scrambling to grab mugs. "I'll make them now."

Patrick gives me a cheeky smirk—like he knows exactly what distracted me.

We each take our coffee and head upstairs toward my dad's office.

We go inside and begin boxing up all of Dad's old work files, organising them so I can easily drop them off at the hospital in case any of the other doctors need them.

I start with the drawers of his desk—folder after folder, every one of them beige, each blending into the next like copies of each other.

Patrick trails his fingers along the dusty bookshelf, stopping on a small framed photo tucked between old novels and a model globe. He picks it up carefully.

It's a picture of me on my tenth birthday, sitting on Dad's shoulders, my face smeared with chocolate cake, both of us laughing at something off-camera.

"This is you," Patrick says gently.

I nod. "Mum always said I was the reason Dad had back problems by the time he was forty."

He smiles, eyes still on the photo. "He looks… so proud."

"He was," I say, voice catching more than I expected it to. "He used to joke that he got a daughter instead of a son because God knew he couldn't handle anyone else stealing the remote."

Patrick chuckles and sets the frame back on the shelf, just as gently as he picked it up.

"He would've liked you," I say before I can stop myself. Patrick looks over at me, surprised.

I shrug. "I don't say that lightly."

He nods, not saying anything, but the way he moves closer says enough.

"I'm glad you're here," I add quietly.

"Me too."

There's a long, soft silence between us. Not uncomfortable— just full of all the things we're both thinking but not quite saying.

Then Patrick turns toward the desk drawers again, and just as I lean over to check the cabinet beneath, I see it:

A bright pink folder, sticking out beneath a stack of beige folders.

"Pink?" I say out loud, frowning. It stands out like a flamingo in a sea of beige. Odd. Why not beige like the others?

I open it, and inside is… another beige folder. But this one's different. This one is labelled:

Lucy's 21st Birthday

My heart skips a beat.

I hesitate, unsure what to do, then slowly lift the beige folder out of the pink one. My fingers tremble slightly as I open it.

Inside are pages—lots of them—and one sealed envelope.

I inhale sharply and let out a long, shaky breath. "What is it?" Patrick asks curiously.

"Um… I'm not sure yet," I say softly, still staring down at the folder. "It has **Lucy's 21st Birthday** written on the front. There's a stack of papers… and an envelope."

Patrick leans over my shoulder, curiosity lighting his face. "Open it," he says gently.

I slide my finger under the flap and pull out the letter inside. The handwriting is instantly familiar.

The paper crinkled between my fingers, and it smelled faintly of my dad's cologne.

To Our Darling Daughter Lucy, Happy 21st Birthday, sweetheart.

We contemplated giving this to you for your 18th, but decided we wanted you to be just a little older before sending you out into the world without us.

Tears prick at my eyes. The words hit harder than they should.

I'm not 21. I'm only 18.

And yet—I've already been sent out into the world without them.

I blink quickly, willing the tears to stay put, and keep reading.

Now that you're 21 and have the world at your feet, it's time to take a leap and see what the world has to offer you. There's enough money for you to take a friend—or someone special.

We've been planning this trip for you for a long time. And now that you're 21, it's time to go.

Travel safe, our girl. Don't forget to take plenty of photos and keep us updated on your whirlwind adventure.

Love always,

Mum and Dad.

The tears fall freely now. I don't bother wiping them away.

The first sheet of paper in the bundle is titled:

6-Month Itinerary

I turn to Patrick, eyes wide, voice shaky.

"They planned to give this to me for my 21st birthday… not knowing they wouldn't be here to get the photos or the updates."

My hands tremble. My parents weren't just planning a vacation—they were handing me a passport to the world.

Patrick looks at me for a long moment, his eyes soft, full of something I can't quite name.

Then, gently, he says, "You have to take this trip. It's what they wanted."

"But I'm not 21 yet," I whisper.

He nods. "Yeah. And your parents aren't here now either. Some things change."

I stare at him, heart pounding.

I hesitate. Is it too soon? Too wild? Asking a guy, I've just met, to spend six months with me.

But when I look at him—really look—I don't see a stranger.

I see someone who feels like a safe place to land. "I'll go… if you come with me."

Without hesitation, he answers, "Yes. Yes, I'll go with you."

My tears of sorrow mix with something else now—hope. Excitement.

I pressed the folder gently closed and set it on the desk, a little more ready to keep going.

We return to packing up the office. The rhythm of sorting and boxing gives me time to process what I've just read, what we've just decided.

A six-month trip. My parents planned this for me, and I had no idea. What were the details? Where were we meant to go?

Once the office is finally packed and all that's left are the furniture pieces, I pick up the folder again—the one that holds the plans for my next adventure—and we head back to the lounge room.

We sit on the couch, the folder between us. I open it, and together, we start flipping through the pages.

I tell Patrick I need to use the bathroom, but in actual fact, I need to message Sienna.

"Hey, I found a bright pink folder in Dad's office."

"Please tell me it's not full of funeral paperwork or old tax returns."

"Worse. Or better? Depends on how you look at it."

"A six-month world trip. They were planning it for my 21st birthday. Tickets, hotel bookings, everything."

"WHAT. Like a whole actual trip?? Like… planes, countries, passports, everything?"

"Yep. The lot."

"Oh my God, Luce… they were giving you the world."

"I know."

"Are you going?"

"Yeah. I need to. For them. For me."

"I mean… hell yes. You should go. But—who's going with you? Or are you solo soul-searching this thing?"

"Patrick."

"Wait. What??"

"We talked. It felt right. I know it sounds crazy."

"You met him, like, five minutes ago. And now you're taking him around the world?"

"I know how it looks. But it doesn't feel crazy. It feels… calm. Like something they'd want for me."

"Okay. As long as you're sure. Just promise me you'll keep your head on while your heart's on fire."

"I promise."

"And text me from every country. With photos. Preferably ones where you're not making out in front of landmarks."

"No promises on that one."

"Ugh. I hate him a little already."

"You'll love him. Eventually."

"I better. Or I'm flying across the world to personally slap some sense into you."

"Love you." "Always."

I close the messages, phone still warm in my hand.

My world cracked wide open the day I lost them. But maybe—just maybe—it's starting to piece itself back together.

Not the same. Never the same.

But something new. Something brave.

They gave me the world. Now it's my turn to go see it.

Chapter 9
Plans And Promises

I can feel the excitement building, and judging by Patrick's face, he feels it too. His eyes are wide with wonder, flicking over each line of the itinerary like a kid reading a treasure map.

"This is insane," he says, laughing. "Six months? Around the world?"

I nod slowly. "It was supposed to be for my twenty-first birthday. A trip with someone special."

He looks up at me, something soft in his expression. "Looks like you found someone special after all."

I try not to melt.

We keep turning the pages, flipping through old plans, hotel reservations, and scribbled notes in the margins. Some pages are printed, others handwritten by my parents. It's all so personal. So real.

I pause when I see it: **Paris**.

"I've always dreamed about making love in Paris," I murmur, not realising the words had escaped aloud.

Patrick chokes on his coffee, then grins. "Looks like your dream might come true."

My eyes go wide, cheeks flushing. "Ahh, sorry. I have a habit of saying things out loud when I shouldn't."

"Don't be sorry, Lucy. Never be sorry for saying what you're thinking."

As we continue reading, we find not only the list of countries we'll be visiting, but detailed plans for what to see and do in each one. It's all here—a six-month journey carefully curated by my parents. A gift I hadn't even known I was still going to receive. And now, with Patrick by my side, it suddenly feels possible.

Six-Month Itinerary

Month 1 – Italy & Greece

Rome, Italy – The Colosseum, Trevi Fountain, Vatican City.

Florence – Renaissance art, leather markets, cooking class. Amalfi Coast – Positano views, cliffside dinners, boat to Capri.

Athens, Greece – Acropolis, taverns with live music.

Santorini–Whitewashed villas, blue domes, candlelit caldera dinner.

Month 2 – Türkiye & Morocco

Istanbul, Türkiye–Hagia Sophia, Grand Bazaar, ferry across the Bosphorus.

Cappadocia – Hot air balloon at sunrise, cave hotel.

Marrakech, Morocco–Spice markets, desert glamping under the stars.

Chefchaouen – The Blue City, quiet alley cafes.

Month 3 – France & Egypt

Paris, France – Eiffel Tower at night, Seine River cruise, Montmartre strolls, and a stay in a charming flat above a bakery.

Cairo, Egypt – Pyramids of Giza, camel ride at sunset.

Nile Cruise – From Luxor to Aswan, temples and ancient ruins.

Month 4 – India & Nepal

Delhi & Agra, India – Taj Mahal visits, a street food tour, and rickshaw rides through bustling markets.

Jaipur – Exploring the Pink City, staying in ornate palaces, and decorating our hands with delicate henna art.

Rishikesh – A yoga retreat by the Ganges, quiet mornings, and deep breaths.

Pokhara, Nepal – Lake views, peaceful hikes through the Annapurna foothills, and moments that feel like stillness wrapped in sunlight.

Month 5 – Japan & South Korea

Kyoto, Japan – Wandering temple paths, admiring cherry blossoms (or autumn leaves), and sipping tea in quiet ceremonies.

Tokyo – Ramen bars, neon-lit culture spots, and one very memorable night in a capsule hotel.

Busan, South Korea – Coastal towns with charm, vibrant seafood markets, and salty air.

Seoul – Historic palaces by day, street food alleys by night, and glittering city views from Namsan Tower.

Month 6 – Bali, Indonesia

Ubud – Lush rice terraces, jungle swings, playful monkeys, and the kind of beauty you feel in your bones.

Seminyak – Beachfront villas, sunset cocktails, and lazy spa days.

Nusa Penida – Snorkeling in clear waters, cliffside photo spots, and quiet hideaways made for dreaming.

Sidemen – A peaceful village retreat to rest, reflect, and prepare for whatever comes next.

"When do we leave?" Patrick asks, excitement buzzing in his voice.

"I'm not sure," I reply, flipping through the last few pages of the travel folder.

There's a name scribbled on a small card tucked in the back pocket. A woman's name—Suzy. Curious, I pick up my phone and dial the number written beneath it.

"Hi, this is Suzy from Travel the World Adventures. How can I help?"

"Um, hi. My name's Lucy. My parents were planning a six-month trip for me for my 21st birthday, but they… passed away recently. I just found a folder with all these details, and your card was inside."

Before I can say anything more, she responds warmly.

"Hi Lucy! I know exactly who you are. I worked closely with your parents to plan this trip. I wasn't sure if you knew about it, but everything is arranged. All I need to know is if you're happy to follow the itinerary, and when you'd like to leave. I'll take care of all the bookings."

Without giving it too much thought, I say, "I can be ready in less than a week."

"Perfect," Suzy replies. "I'll finalise everything just as your parents requested. I'll email you the details by Friday. Be ready to leave Monday."

I hang up and turn to Patrick. "We leave Monday."

"Today's Wednesday," he says, eyebrows raised.

A sudden wave of nerves crashes over me. My thoughts spiral. My mouth starts moving faster than my brain.

"There's so much to organise. Packing… clothes… oh God, what do I pack? Lingerie! I need lingerie—"

"Lingerie, huh?" Patrick grins. "Top of the packing list?"

"Oh crap," I mumble, covering my face. "There I go again… thinking out loud."

He leans back casually, not missing a beat. "Well, what's at the top of my list? Condoms."

I blink. We haven't really discussed having sex with each other—only our lack of it with anyone else. But now that we're about to spend six months travelling together, I guess… we probably should.

We sit quietly for a moment, staring into each other's eyes, filled with excitement and something deeper. Something real.

"We should probably have the talk," I say.

"You're right," he replies. "Are you on the pill?"

"Yeah, I am. And since neither of us has been with anyone else, we should be fine without… you know."

"Good," he says. "I've heard it feels better without them anyway."

I laugh. "Well, that's one less thing you have to pack."

We both glance at the time and realise how late it's gotten.

"I should probably head home," Patrick says. "We completely lost track of time. Maybe I should go pack tonight and come back tomorrow? We should probably get a couple of days together before we commit to six months straight."

"Good idea," I agree, walking him to the door.

The moonlight casts a silver glow across his face—he looks almost ethereal. He leans in and presses a gentle kiss to my forehead.

Wait… my forehead?

Before I can ask why, he softly says, "If I kiss your lips, I won't be able to leave."

I smirk, heart pounding. "I understand. And I feel the same."

Instead, I take a deep breath and smile. "Goodnight, Patrick. See you tomorrow."

He walks off into the night, I close the door behind him and immediately call Sienna.

She answers on the second ring.

"Luce? What's wrong?"

I smile at her immediate concern. "Nothing's wrong. I just… need your help."

"You found another pink folder?"

I laugh. "No. But we leave Monday."

There's a beat of silence, and then— "Holy shit, you're actually doing it?"

"We? As in… you and Lover Boy?"

"Patrick. And yes."

She lets out a squeal that makes me pull the phone away from my ear.

"This is insane! I'm packing for you already—in my head, you'll need comfy shoes, travel-size shampoo, that sexy black jumpsuit, and your pill, maybe even condoms."

I choke. "Excuse me?"

"What? You're going around the world with a man who kisses you and fireworks explode. Don't pretend you're not going to need them."

"Sienna!"

"Tell me I'm wrong."

"…You're not, but we talked and no condoms, just my pill."

"I hope you know what you're doing, I'll be over tomorrow morning with coffee, a playlist, and aggressive packing energy."

"Thank God."

"And Lucy?"

"Yeah?"

"I'm proud of you. This isn't just a trip. This is you choosing life again. They'd be so damn proud."

My throat tightens. "I hope so."

"I know so. Now go to sleep. Big day tomorrow. Also… pack the red lace. You'll thank me later."

I laugh, tears in my eyes. "Love you."

"Always. Night, world traveller."

I head upstairs and collapse into bed, heart full, mind racing. But tonight…

Tonight it feels like I'm lying on a cloud. Thinking about all that lies ahead…And the holiday I'll never forget.

Chapter 10

All In

I wake early, my mind already racing. It's Thursday. We leave on Monday.

There's still so much to do—but first things first: shopping.

I spent the entire day with Sienna moving from store to store, building an almost completely new wardrobe. Jeans, tops, dresses, jumpers, heels, flats, joggers—and, of course, lingerie. Lots of lingerie.

By the time I get home, the excitement has me buzzing. I throw my bags onto the bed and start packing, but halfway through, I decide to shower and get ready.

Just in case… tonight is the night.

My imagination runs wild again, picturing what might be under Patrick's shirt… and even more under his pants. But somehow, I manage to focus long enough to actually get ready.

I shower, shave—everything, everywhere—and wash my hair. I blow-dry and straighten it to silky perfection. A little makeup, a soft spritz of perfume, and then I slip into the little black number I bought today.

Underneath it: lacy black lingerie I'd barely had the courage to buy.

Just as I reach for something to throw on over the top, the doorbell rings.

Panic. I grab the oversized T-shirt already lying on my bed and throw it on as I head for the stairs.

I glance at myself in the mirror one last time and grab my phone for Sienna's reassurance.

"What if I chicken out?"

"You shaved EVERYTHING. It's too late to back out now."

"That's fair."

I laugh and toss the phone on the bed. Too late now.

I open the door, hesitating, what if I'm not good enough?

What if it's awkward?

Patrick's eyes scan me slowly, and he grins. "Wow. I don't know how long I can wait to find out what's under that shirt."

I laugh. "I didn't get time to fully dress. I spent the whole day shopping."

"All day, huh?" His eyes twinkle. "You must've tried on every piece of lingerie in the store."

Truthfully, I just grabbed what looked sexy and made a run for it. But he doesn't need to know that.

He leans in. "What colour are you wearing now?"

I smile, lowering my voice. "Play your cards right, and you might find out."

The second the words leave my lips, he moves. Fast.

Patrick lifts me by the waist, my legs instinctively wrapping around him. He kicks the door closed behind us and pins me gently against it.

"My cards are all on the table, Lucy," he whispers in my ear. "I want you. Now. I don't want to wait another minute."

I'm breathless, shaking—but not from nerves. "Take me upstairs," I whisper back.

He carries me effortlessly up the stairs, strong and sure. At the top, he places me gently in front of my bed.

"I want to lay you down," he says, "but first... I need to see what's under the shirt."

Slowly, teasingly, I lift the oversized T-shirt, revealing the barely-there lingerie underneath.

His eyes widen. "Wow."

He steps forward, fingertips trailing down my arms before reaching around to undo the single clasp. The fabric slides from my body, leaving me completely exposed.

And yet—I've never felt so comfortable.

"So," I murmur, raising an eyebrow, "why am I the only one

naked?"

Without hesitation, Patrick strips down. No shame. No hesitation. Just confidence.

Now we're both standing there—naked. Gazing at each other. And yes, letting our eyes wander.

I step toward him, dropping to my knees, my eyes locking with his.

He's even bigger than I imagined—hard, thick, pulsing with heat and want, it's perfect. I run my tongue slowly around him, letting my mouth glide up and down.

His hands thread into my hair, gentle but encouraging, a low moan escaping his lips.

I taste him slowly, letting my lips explore every inch, then I take him into my mouth, each and every inch of him.

After a moment, he urges me up, lifting me effortlessly and laying me on the bed.

His lips meet mine, then trail downward—my neck, my chest, each breast receiving attention that leaves me breathless.

I can feel him pressed hard against me as he moves lower, his hands parting my thighs.

When his mouth finds me, I nearly lose my mind.

His tongue moves with purpose—slow, teasing strokes that make me arch into him. I moan. Loudly. And I hear him moan, too.

Patrick lifts his head and meets my eyes.

"I want to feel inside you," he says softly. "But not just with my fingers. I want all of you."

I reach for him, pulling his face to mine. "I want you, Patrick. Now."

"I'll go slow," he promises. And he does.

He slides into me inch by inch, slow and steady. Our eyes lock, watching every expression on each other's faces, memorising this moment.

When he's fully inside me, he holds still for a moment—buried deep—his breath ragged as he gazes down at me like he's barely holding it together.

"Are you okay?" he asks, voice husky, trembling with restraint. I nod, chest heaving. "More than okay. Please… don't stop."

He pulls back slowly, almost all the way out, then slides back in with exquisite control. I gasp, fingers clutching the sheets, the stretch and fullness dizzying. He moves again—slow, deep strokes that make my body sing, rolling his hips with rhythm that feels deliberate, practiced, reverent.

Every thrust hits that perfect spot inside me, drawing breathy moans from my lips. His pelvis grinds against mine just enough to send sparks dancing through me. The friction, the pressure, the weight of him above me—it's overwhelming in the best way.

His hands slide under my thighs, lifting and angling me just enough for him to go deeper. My legs wrap around his waist instinctively, holding him there, needing more.

"God, Lucy," he groans into my neck. "You feel… fucking incredible."

His pace builds—still controlled, but rougher now, each thrust slamming into the deepest parts of me. The sound of skin meeting skin, of breath and whimpers and need, fills the room. I can feel myself unravelling. My body coils tighter with every stroke, every grind of his hips, every whispered groan against my skin.

"Something's happening," I gasp, the tension snapping tight inside me. "Oh my God—Patrick—"

He grips my hips and drives into me, relentless and deep. "You're about to come. Let go. I've got you."

And so I let go.

My body erupts, back arching violently off the bed as pleasure crashes over me, white-hot, all-consuming. My orgasm rips through me, stealing my breath as I cry out his name.

And just as my body starts to come down, I feel him shudder.

He drives in hard one last time, groaning low and guttural as he releases deep inside me. His body goes rigid above mine, his mouth falling open in a moan that makes my pulse spike all over again.

He collapses against me, our slick skin pressed together, both of us panting, drenched in sweat and trembling.

Still inside me.

Still mine.

His lips find my shoulder. A soft kiss. A quiet hum. "Holy fuck," he whispers.

I can't speak. I can barely move. But in this moment—completely undone and held in his arms—I've never felt more alive.

Patrick brushes the hair from my face and whispers, "I want to do that with you every day for the rest of my life." I can't speak. I just smile and nod, still trembling from the intensity.

He pulls me into his arms, and we both lay there, heartbeats still pounding.

"Was it what you imagined?" he asks quietly, brushing his thumb across my cheek.

I smile, eyes heavy. "It was more. Because it was you."

We don't talk much after that—just soft kisses, shared breaths, and that warm hum of something real settling between us.

Wrapped in his embrace, content, full, completely his and for the first time in what feels like forever, I don't feel haunted. I feel wanted. Safe. Seen.

This isn't just a night. This is the start of something.

And as my body melts into his, I know with absolute certainty…

I made the right choice, inviting him into my world.

I drift off to sleep—I know my first time was definitely a moment I'll never forget.

Chapter 11
Wheels Up, Hearts Full

On Friday, we continued getting ready for our trip, spending countless hours scrolling through the computer and looking at all the places my parents had chosen for us to go. The final itinerary and all the relevant booking information from Suzy— including our flight details—came through.

"I've never been on a plane before. I've never left this town," Patrick says, his voice carrying a nervous edge.

"I've only flown once, to New Zealand with my parents," I reply.

Patrick notices the booking details. "What the… First class?"

"Seriously, would you expect anything less from my parents?" I say with a laugh. He glances around my house and shrugs. "Yeah, I guess not."

As the days roll by, our excitement builds—and so does our intimacy. We've had sex in almost every room of the house. By Sunday night, we're packing the last of our things, knowing we have to be at the airport early the next morning.

I head for the shower and turn on the water, letting the steam slowly fill the room. The heat rises quickly, wrapping around me like a blanket. My skin begins to flush, glowing red under the spray as the tension of the day melts from my muscles.

Just as I close my eyes and tilt my head back, I hear his voice. "Can I join you?"

"Sure."

A flutter of nerves hits my stomach. Shower sex—somehow, we hadn't ticked that one off the list yet. And the thought of him naked, wet, and pressed up against me under the stream is almost too much to bear.

I hear the soft thud of his clothes hitting the floor, one by one. My breath catches. A second later, the shower door opens.

Patrick steps inside, steam rising between us, beads of water already clinging to his skin. His hair is wet, dripping down his temples, and his eyes darken as they meet mine.

He closes the distance between us in one slow step, his hand reaching out to cup the back of my neck as he leans in to kiss me, slow and deliberate, like he has all the time in the world to explore my mouth. The water cascades over us, slicking our bodies together.

He presses me gently against the cool tile wall, one hand sliding down to lift my thigh over his hip. I feel him hard and ready between my legs, his breath hot against my cheek.

"Tell me you want this," he whispers.

"I want this. I want you."

In one smooth, strong motion, he lifts me fully, wrapping my legs around his waist. The head of him nudges against me, and then he's inside, deep, thick, stretching me with every inch. I gasp, clinging to his shoulders as he fills me.

"God," he groans, his lips brushing my ear.

"You feel… incredible."

The rhythm starts slow, teasing. His hips roll against mine, the water running down his back, our skin slick and sliding. My back arches with each thrust, the pressure of the wall behind me grounding me as my body spirals into heat.

He lowers his head, sucking gently at the curve of my neck, then moving to my breasts, licking and biting until I moan so loudly it echoes against the tiles.

My fingers grip the back of his neck, holding on as the rhythm builds—faster, deeper. Each thrust hits the perfect spot, and my moans mix with his as the pressure builds inside me.

"You like that?" he pants.

"Yes. More—don't stop."

He doesn't. The wet slap of our bodies, the steam fogging up the glass, the slippery, unrelenting pleasure—it's everything.

"I'm so close," I whisper.

"I can feel you," he says, his breath rough. "Let go for me."

I come undone with a cry, my body tensing, pulsing around him. He follows seconds later, slamming into me with one final thrust before groaning into my neck as he releases inside me.

He holds me there, both of us gasping, hearts racing. Slowly, gently, he lowers me to the floor, brushing wet hair from my face.

"You okay?" he whispers, lips brushing my forehead.

"I've never been better."

Patrick reaches for the shampoo, lathering it gently into my hair. I close my eyes and lean into his touch, savouring the tenderness. It's not rushed. It's not just sex. It's care. Connection.

He rinses my hair, then reaches for a cloth, washing every inch of me with the same patience and attention, like I'm something precious.

By the time he finishes, I'm not just clean—I'm completely unravelled.

Once we're fully rinsed and wrapped in towels, we crawl into bed and fall asleep in each other's arms, the alarm already set for 5:00 a.m.

Beep. Beep. Beep.

I shoot out of bed faster than ever. The excitement—and nerves—take over. Patrick wakes more slowly, blinking in the soft light.

"We need to hurry," I say, already grabbing my clothes.

"We've got to be at the airport in two hours."

Patrick zips up the suitcase and drops it by the door. "That's the last of it," he says, wiping his hands on his jeans. "Can you believe we're actually doing this?"

I nod, smiling — but it's tight. My chest has been heavy all morning, and it's not just the weight of the packing.

Patrick notices. Of course he does.

"You've been weird since breakfast," he says gently. "Is everything okay?" I hesitate. Say it, Lucy.

"I lied to you," I blurt, the words sharp in the air. "About Zeke."

Patrick stills, his brow knitting. "What do you mean?"

"You asked me if I'd messaged him after our dinner. I said no. And that part was true… but I didn't tell you he showed up. That night. He was waiting on my doorstep when I got home."

Patrick's jaw tenses. He doesn't say anything right away.

I rush to fill the silence. "I didn't tell you because I didn't want to ruin what we had just started. I didn't know how to explain it without making it sound like more than it was."

"What did he want?"

"To know if I was sleeping with you," I say bluntly. "To tell me he missed me. To make me doubt myself."

"And did you?" Patrick asks, his voice calm but low.

I meet his eyes. "No. But I doubted myself. I felt guilty for being happy, for letting someone in. And I didn't want that to leak into this. Into you."

He takes a slow breath and nods.

"I wish you'd told me," he says finally. "But I get it. I really do."

Relief and shame twist inside me. "I'm sorry."

Patrick steps closer, his hand brushing my cheek. "It's okay to still be untangling things, Lucy. Just don't do it alone, yeah?"

I nod, blinking back the sudden sting in my eyes.

"We're good," he says softly. "But if he shows up again— next time, tell me."

"I will."

And I mean it.

During the drive to the airport, we talk about all the things we're excited for—and all the adventures that lie ahead.

At the airport, we park the car, grab our bags, and head inside. "Oh great, here comes the security screening."

"Ma'am, I'm going to need you to remove your shoes," the security agent said flatly.

I grumbled, wobbling slightly as I slipped out of my boots.

"This is the least sexy part of travel," I muttered to Patrick.

"Speak for yourself," he whispered. "Watching you awkwardly hop on one foot is oddly adorable."

"If I fall and flash everyone, it's on you."

"I'll take the blame—and the front row seat."

The terminal is huge, but we manage to find our way to the First-Class lounge. As we wait for our flight, the conversation continues, my emotions all over the place.

I can't help but think about my parents and how they planned this trip for me. And now, not only am I taking it as they hoped—I'm taking it with someone special. Someone, I think, I'm falling for.

My emotions run high, and I realise that in the chaos of the morning—well, the last few days—I forgot to text Sienna.

I find a quiet corner by the departure gate while Patrick grabs us coffee. My phone **buzzes**. It's Sienna.

Sienna: *"Please tell me you're not about to get on a 24-hour flight without one last confession."*

I smile and call her instead. "Hey," I say.

"Girl. Tell me everything. You're leaving the country with a man who turned your white bra see-through on day one. I deserve DETAILS."

I laugh. "You already know the important part."

"Sure, but now I need intimate intel. Are we talking lights-off respectful missionary, or throw-you-against-the-wall? 'I'll replace the drywall later' kind of energy?"

"Oh my God, Sienna." "You're not denying it."

I glance around, lowering my voice. "Let's just say… I've been thoroughly distracted."

"I knew it. That boy has 'I read romance novels for research' energy."

"And surprisingly gentle hands."

Sienna squeals. "Okay, now I hate him a little less."

I pause. "Also… I told him. About Zeke. The doorstep. Lying about it."

She quiets for a beat. "How'd he takes it?"

"Better than I deserved. He was calm. Said he got it. That he wished I'd told him sooner, but… he understood."

"Well, shit," she says softly. "Sounds like he might actually be a decent human."

"I think he is." Another pause.

"Are you scared?" she asks gently.

"A little. But not of him. Just… of everything changing. Of who I'll be when I come back."

"You'll be you," she says. "Just more… worldly and probably very well-sexed."

"You're impossible."

"You love me."

"I do."

"Good," she says. "Now go fall in love with a country. And maybe with him a little."

I glance toward the boarding gate as Patrick returns, coffee in hand and that warm look in his eyes. "Gotta go. Love you."

"Always."

Just as I hang up, Patrick hands me my coffee. "Who was that? Who do you love?"

I shake my head and smirk at him. "It was Sienna wishing us a wonderful trip."

He knows that's not all the conversation was about, but takes my answer as girl talk and leaves it at that.

We board the plane and settle into our spacious first-class seats. Just as we're about to take off, Patrick reaches for my hand.

I think he's a little scared of flying, but I squeeze his hand

and smile.

"Hey Patrick, the next time we have sex, it'll be in another country."

His eyes widen, and he laughs. "Hey Lucy, I'm going to have sex with you in every country."

I laugh with him as the plane lifts into the sky. He squeezes my hand until we level out.

"Now it's time to sit back and relax… until we land in Italy."

As the plane cruised above the clouds, Patrick drifted off beside me, his hand still loosely holding mine.

Then I turned my face toward the window, watching the stars blink through the haze. A wave of emotion rolled through me—grief, gratitude, nerves, and something that felt suspiciously like love.

My parents would've loved this moment. They would've teased me for being sentimental, for crying while the world opened up beneath me.

"I miss you," I whispered to the sky. "But I promise—I'll live this trip for both of you."

Chapter 12

Wishes And Whispers

As our plane touches down in Italy, Patrick and I make our way through the bustling airport to collect our bags. He glances at me, excitement lighting up his face.

"Hey, I don't speak any language other than English. What about you?"

I laugh. "Nope. This trip is going to be interesting."

Bags in hand, we exit the airport and wave down the first cab we see. I show the driver a piece of paper with our hotel name printed on it. He nods.

"Good morning, my name's Will. I'll drive you to your hotel. It's only about twenty minutes from here."

I raise an eyebrow at the name that clearly doesn't match his thick Italian accent or appearance. But I just smile and nod. Patrick chuckles beside me.

The drive into the city leaves us both breathless—winding streets, ancient buildings, the romantic chaos of Rome unfolding around us. We pass a charming restaurant, its tables set beneath twinkling fairy lights.

"We're eating there tonight," I whisper.

"Deal," Patrick replies.

We arrive at our hotel, and Will hands me a card with his number. "If you want to see Italy in all its glory, call me. I'll show you around."

I thank him and pocket the card. Inside the hotel, we step into the lobby and both gasp. The photos online didn't do it justice—marble floors, crystal chandeliers, and the scent of fresh roses in the air. We're checked in within minutes and escorted to our suite.

The door clicks open and we step into the suite. Floor-to-ceiling windows flood the space with late-afternoon sun. A velvet chaise lounge sits by the window, and a welcome tray with fruit, cheese, and a bottle of chilled Prosecco waits on the table.

I drop my bag, staring at the view. "This doesn't feel real." Patrick walks to the window, pulls back the curtain further, and whistles. "It's like living in a painting."

I pour us each a glass of Prosecco, hand him one, and clink lightly. "To firsts. First time in Rome, first hotel together…"

He grins. "Did you see the size of the bed? it is easily the biggest I've ever seen, we could have some serious fun on that."

I laugh, "Later. First—food."

We freshen up quickly, then stroll hand in hand to the restaurant we saw earlier. As we walk, we're surrounded by the golden hues of the setting sun against old stone buildings, cobbled streets, and blooming balconies. It's like stepping into a dream.

Inside the restaurant, we're seated by a large window with a direct view of the Trevi Fountain. The sound of water mingles with soft violin music playing somewhere nearby.

I nod toward the fountain. "That's our next stop. It's on my parents' list. They left me a note about it: Throw a coin in the fountain and make a wish. But seal your lips afterwards and never tell a soul."

We order pasta, fresh bread, and sparkling wine. It's the most delicious meal I've ever tasted. Every bite is perfect.

After dinner, we wander toward the Trevi Fountain. It's even more stunning up close. The lights shimmer in the cascading water, and dozens of people are throwing coins, taking photos, or simply staring in awe.

I pull two coins from my pocket and hand one to Patrick. "Here—make a wish. But don't tell."

He smiles, and we both close our eyes and toss the coins into the water.

"So… what did you wish for?" he asks, nudging me. I grin.

"Can't say. It won't come true."

But in my heart, I already know: my wish is standing right in front of me.

We head back to the hotel to spend our first night in Italy. I close the door behind us. "Make sure to lock it."

Patrick turns to face me, his eyes locked on mine, his voice low and hoarse. "You okay?"

I nod, heart pounding. "More than okay."

He crosses the space between us slowly, like he's giving me time to run. But I don't want to run. Not tonight.

"I've wanted to touch you since the moment we landed," he murmurs, brushing his knuckles down my cheek. "But you looked so damn beautiful… I didn't want to rush anything."

"You're not rushing," I whisper, heat blooming under my skin.

He pulls me into him, hands at my waist, his mouth finding mine in a kiss that's slow, sure, and absolutely lethal. He takes his time, letting it build—his tongue brushing mine, his hands exploring like he's learning a language written only in my body.

"I need you," I breathe, tugging at the hem of his shirt.

He lets me strip it over his head. He's golden in the low light, every muscle defined, every inch of him carved like a statue— except warm, alive, hungry.

I barely have time to react before he scoops me up and carries me across the suite, laying me gently on the impossibly large bed. He kneels beside me, fingers sliding up my legs with slow reverence, pushing my dress up until it's bunched around my hips.

He groans. "You're not wearing a bra."

"Maybe I had plans."

"I love your plans."

His mouth trails down my neck, licking and kissing every inch. His hands skim over my breasts, fingers circling my nipples until they harden beneath his touch. Then he slides lower, pressing a kiss to my belly before hooking his thumbs into my underwear.

With one last look for permission, he tugs them down slowly, letting them slide over my thighs and knees and off.

He pauses.

"You're so fucking beautiful, Lucy."

His mouth finds my inner thigh, lips dragging across my skin as he moves closer to where I need him. When his tongue finally flicks across my centre, I cry out, arching into him. He moans against me like he's starved for the taste, his fingers digging into my hips to hold me still as he devours me.

My hands twist in the sheets, my thighs trembling as he brings me to the edge, pulls me back, then pushes me over again. I gasp his name, a stuttered plea falling from my lips as I shatter against his mouth.

He kisses his way back up, lips swollen, eyes dark. I tug at his belt, unfastening his jeans and pushing them down. He sheds them in seconds, revealing all of him—hard, thick, perfect.

I reach for him, wrapping my hand around him, stroking

slowly. He groans, forehead resting on mine, like the moment might undo him.

"I can't wait," he murmurs. "I need to be inside you."

"Then stop waiting." I whisper. "I want to feel you."

He slides into me slowly, watching every reaction on my face. Inch by inch, he fills me until I'm gasping, stretching around him. He stills, giving us both a moment to adjust.

"God, you feel so good," he breathes. "So tight, so warm…"

He begins to move, slow, controlled thrusts that leave me clawing at his back. Each roll of his hips hits deeper, harder, and I moan into his mouth as he kisses me again, swallowing every sound I make.

Our bodies move together in a rhythm that's both frantic and tender. His hands roam everywhere—my waist, my thighs, my breasts—like he wants to remember how I feel from every angle.

"Patrick," I gasp, nails digging into his shoulders. "Don't stop."

"I'm not going anywhere," he growls, driving into me harder now.

Heat coils in my belly, spiraling out of control. I feel myself building, tightening, about to snap.

"Fuck—Lucy—" he pants. "Come with me."

And then I do—my orgasm crashes through me like a tidal

wave. My back arches, a raw cry torn from my throat as pleasure floods every nerve.

He follows seconds later, a guttural groan spilling from his chest as he comes inside me, his entire body tensing, then trembling as he collapses gently against me.

For a long while, we just breathe. His weight on me is grounding. His skin is hot against mine, his heartbeat thundering where our chests touch.

Patrick lifts his head, brushing damp hair from my face. "That… that was more than I imagined. That… was definitely a moment I'll never forget."

I smile, still breathless. "Me too."

The next few days in Italy pass in a blur of beauty and wonder. We explore the Colosseum, wander through the Vatican Museums, and get lost in Trastevere's charming alleys. One afternoon, we accidentally hop on the wrong tram and end up in a tiny neighbourhood market where no one speaks English.

"Guess we're learning Italian the hard way," Patrick laughs, holding up a mystery pastry.

It turns out to be filled with olives and cheese. We buy two more.

Our nights are filled with laughter, kisses, and soft moans behind closed doors. We make love like time doesn't exist, like the world outside our suite has faded away.

And every morning in Rome, we explore. We stood in awe beneath the towering arches of the Colosseum, wandered through the echoing halls of Vatican City and moved slowly through the Vatican Museums, I paused in front of a massive fresco. Patrick was standing behind me, arms loosely wrapped around my waist, chin resting on my shoulder.

"My mum would have loved this," I whispered.

Patrick doesn't say anything. He just holds me tighter. And in that moment, I swear I feel her with me. We moved down through cobblestone alleys where locals sip espresso and life moves slower.

In Florence, we wandered through Renaissance galleries until the marble statues blurred into something dreamlike, strolled through the leather markets while Patrick tried (and failed) to haggle, and signed up for a cooking class where I proved—once again—that I'm better at eating pasta than making it. He teased me about nearly setting the sauce on fire for days.

We let ourselves exhale on the Amalfi Coast. Days were filled with cliffside seafood lunches, late-night gelato runs, and boat rides to Capri, where we swam in crystal blue water and kissed under the sun. Every sunset felt like it was made just for us.

In Athens, we climbed the worn steps of the Acropolis and watched the world stretch out beneath ancient marble. Then we chased music into back-alley taverns, where the wine flowed freely and we danced to rhythms we didn't know—but didn't need to understand.

And then came Santorini.

It was like stepping into a postcard—all whitewashed walls, blue domes, and cascading bougainvillea. I'd seen photos before, but they never quite captured the feeling of being there—of the breeze off the sea, the soft crunch of stone underfoot, the weightless quiet of twilight.

On our last night, we shared a candlelit dinner on a private terrace overlooking the caldera. Patrick reached across the table and laced his fingers with mine like it was second nature.

I looked around at the sea, the stars, and him—and for the first time in a long time, I didn't feel like I was standing in someone else's life.

This was mine.

And I was finally starting to live it.

Back at our villa, I step onto the balcony while Patrick finishes brushing his teeth. The sky is painted in streaks of pink and gold, the sun slowly sinking behind the caldera.

Patrick joins me a moment later, a soft towel slung around his shoulders. He wraps his arms around me from behind, resting his chin on my head.

"This place," I whisper. "I could stay here forever."

"Then let's never leave," he murmurs.

I smile. "You say that now, but wait till you see what's next."

"Doesn't matter where we go," he says. "If you're there, I want to be too."

Chapter 13
Moments In Colour

Istanbul was chaos and beauty in equal measure. The call to prayer echoed over the city as we stepped out of our hotel that first morning, hand in hand, ready to lose ourselves in the ancient streets.

We wandered through the Grand Bazaar, weaving between stalls bursting with silks, spices, and glittering lanterns. Patrick bartered clumsily, charming every vendor, while I stocked up on rose tea and evil eye trinkets. The scent of cinnamon and cardamom clung to our clothes as we stepped out of the Grand Bazaar, I caught Patrick watching me, not the stalls or the trinkets, but me.

"What?" I ask, tucking a strand of hair behind my ear.

He shrugs, then says, "You just… fit here. Like you belong."

"Covered in spices and surrounded by chaos?" I laugh.

"No," he says, stepping closer. "Alive. I've never seen your eyes shine like this."

And maybe it's the charm of Istanbul, or the weight of his words, but for the first time since losing them, I feel it too. Like I'm stepping back into my skin.

As we step into the cool, cavernous Hagia Sophia. I watched

Patrick look up in awe at the golden dome, and it hit me all over again—we were really here. Living this.

We took a ferry across the Bosphorus, sailing between two continents. He wrapped his arms around me from behind, and I leaned into him, watching the city sprawl along the shore as the wind tangled my hair. It was peaceful. Perfect.

Then came Cappadocia.

We woke before dawn, bundled in layers as we climbed into a hot air balloon. The sky slowly shifted from ink to lavender to gold. As we floated above the honeycomb landscape, dozens of other balloons rose around us like paper lanterns. It was silent up there, just the occasional burst of flame above our heads and Patrick's breath in my ear as he whispered, "This is unreal."

That night, we stayed in a cave hotel. Warm lights danced over ancient stone walls, and I don't know if it was the altitude, the wine, or just the way he looked at me, but I needed him.

We barely made it through the doorway before I pressed him against the wall, pulling his jacket off and letting it fall to the floor. He spun me around and carried me to the bed, laying me down on the thick embroidered quilt like I was something sacred.

His touch was slower this time. Like he was memorising me. My skin burned under his fingers, and every kiss felt like a vow. I arched beneath him, whispering his name like a prayer. We moved together, wrapped in velvet shadows, the quiet echo of our moans against the stone walls the only sound. It was a rhythm—slow, deep, unhurried—until we were both trembling, clinging to each other in the stillness that followed.

Afterwards, he brushed a strand of hair from my face and kissed my shoulder.

"I don't ever want to forget this," he whispered.

"You won't," I whispered back. "It's a moment we'll never forget."

We left Türkiye with sand still clinging to our boots and the scent of saffron in our bags, bound for Morocco.

Marrakech was wild—a blur of snake charmers, spinning lanterns, and the hypnotic pulse of drums. We explored the Medina, getting lost in its twisting alleys and spice-scented air. I bought a velvet robe in a deep emerald green. Patrick said I looked like a queen.

We spent the night glamping in the desert under a sky littered with stars. There was no noise. No light. Just the crackle of a fire, the feel of him wrapped around me in the tent, and the way his lips found mine in the hush of night.

Then came Chefchaouen—the Blue City. Quiet. Dreamlike.

The buildings were every shade of blue imaginable, from cornflower to cobalt. We drank mint tea at a cafe tucked into a quiet alleyway, our knees brushing under the table. He reached for my hand, and we just sat there in silence, smiling.

It was a slower kind of magic—one that settled deep into your bones. One that didn't need fireworks to feel real.

And for the first time in my life… I didn't feel like I was running anymore.

I was right where I wanted to be.

Paris was everything I dreamed it would be—and somehow even more.

We stayed in a tiny flat tucked above a corner bakery in Montmartre, where the scent of fresh croissants drifted through the window every morning. The streets felt like something out of a movie, all soft light, cobblestones, and quiet cafes with tiny tables made for lingering.

We visited all the classics—stood beneath the Eiffel Tower, wandered hand in hand through the Louvre, and kissed on a nighttime Seine River cruise as the lights of Paris shimmered on the water.

One evening, we took a bottle of red wine up to the Sacré-Cœur steps and watched the city lights stretch out before us. Paris didn't just sparkle—it pulsed with a kind of magic that wrapped itself around us.

As we descend the steps of Sacré-Cœur, I paused to look back at the view—Paris stretching wide beneath us like a living painting. Patrick wraps his arm around my shoulders.

"This city is dangerous," he murmurs.

"Why?"

"Because it makes you believe in forever."

I glance up at him. "Do you?"

He looks down, eyes steady. "I'm starting to."

My heart stumbles in my chest. I don't say anything. I just hold his hand tighter.

Later that night, we returned to our flat, laughter still clinging to our lips like the last notes of a love song. The glow from the streetlamp outside cast a golden haze across the room, soft and flickering, like candlelight.

Patrick closed the door behind us, his eyes on me, not hungry, but full. Full of something that felt too big for words.

He didn't speak. He just stepped close and cupped my face, his thumb brushing slowly across my cheek like he was memorising me by touch.

"You're beautiful," he whispered.

I smiled, but it wavered. "You always say that when the lights are low."

"Because that's when the truth speaks loudest," he said, voice steady.

He kissed me then, slow and deep. Not urgent, not rushed. Just careful. His lips pressed to mine like a promise. Each movement felt like a question, and each sigh, an answer.

We undressed each other quietly, carefully, as if the sound of a zipper might break the moment. My dress slipped from my shoulders, pooling at my feet. His shirt followed, his body warm as he pulled me against him.

We slipped between the sheets, skin to skin, breath to breath. He traced slow circles on my hip with his thumb, his eyes never leaving mine.

"Are you sure?" he asked. I nodded, unable to speak.

When he entered me, it wasn't with heat or hunger, but with something steadier. It felt like being known. Like he was listening with his body instead of words.

We moved together slowly, like a tide rising and falling.

Every touch was soft. Every kiss, a quiet discovery.

He kissed my forehead, my jaw, the hollow of my throat. I whispered his name into the space between our lips, over and over, like I was afraid the night might forget it.

Our bodies found a rhythm so tender it ached, not from pain, but from everything it meant.

He stilled, just for a second, forehead pressed to mine. Our breaths tangled, our hearts steady.

He didn't speak. He just kissed me again—deeper, slower, as if he was trying to etch this moment into both of us.

And when we both came, it was silent. No gasps, no cries— just a shudder, a soft exhale, and the hush of something new settling into the space between us.

He wrapped himself around me, our limbs entwined, our bodies still slick and warm. Outside, Paris breathed around us.

I lay there, eyes wide open, heart cracked cleanly in two. Neither of us spoke.

We didn't have to.

Neither of us knew that something had just begun—A piece of him had just taken root inside me. A new heartbeat would echo from this night.

From the romance of Paris, we flew into the chaos and wonder of Cairo.

The heat hit us the second we stepped off the plane—thick and dry, like we were walking into history. And in a way, we were.

Standing before the Pyramids of Giza, I felt tiny like a speck in the timeline of something so ancient and sacred. Patrick reached for my hand as we rode camels into the sunset, the silhouettes of the pyramids stretching long and golden behind us.

After a few days in the city, we boarded a river cruise down the Nile, and time seemed to melt completely. We drifted past temples and tombs, from Luxor to Aswan, where ancient hieroglyphs told stories older than anything we'd ever known.

It was like touching eternity—with him by my side.

We made love slowly, reverently, under linen sheets as the boat rocked gently down the river, surrounded by silence and stars.

The next morning, I woke early to the soft lapping of water and golden sunlight spilling through our cabin windows. Patrick is still asleep beside me, one arm flung across my waist, his chest rising and falling in slow, peaceful rhythm.

I lie there watching him—memorising the curve of his jaw, the faint stubble, the quiet strength in his face even at rest.

How did I get here?

From grief, to this bed. From silence, to this love.

I press a soft kiss to his shoulder and whisper, "Thank you."

Not just for this moment. But for helping me feel again.

Travelling like this wasn't just about seeing the world anymore.

It was about creating a new one together.

And in every step, every kiss, every quiet morning… the chaos and beauty of life wove us into something whole again.

Chapter 14

Holding Hair, Holding Hearts

We landed in Delhi under a heavy sky—the kind that wrapped the city in heat and haze. Stepping outside the airport, the air felt thick with spice, honking horns, and the energy of a place that pulsed with life. It was overwhelming and beautiful all at once.

Patrick clutched his backpack, wide-eyed. "I don't even know where to look first."

We checked into a boutique hotel tucked behind bustling streets. The staff welcomed us with cool drinks and marigold garlands. I smiled, but a wave of nausea rolled through me. I chalked it up to the long flight and the heat.

Later, we joined a guided street food tour. The smells were intoxicating—spicy chaat, hot samosas, mango lassis. Patrick tried everything. I nibbled, but my appetite wasn't there. Still, I laughed when he tried to out-spice the locals and lost miserably.

In Agra, the Taj Mahal shimmered at sunrise. We stood barefoot on the white marble, hand in hand. I wanted to take it all in—the beauty, the stillness, the love that built something so timeless. But as we walked through the gardens, the heat climbed, and dizziness hit me like a wave. I had to sit.

That evening, on a rickshaw ride back from the market, the nausea turned violent. As soon as we got back to our hotel, I was in the bathroom, heaving.

Patrick was there instantly. He knelt beside me, pulling back my hair gently. "Bad food?" he asked softly.

I wiped my mouth and forced a smile. "Maybe. Or jet lag. Or… maybe something else."

We exchanged a look—unspoken but loud.

In Jaipur, we stayed in a restored palace. The pink walls and ornate arches looked like something out of a dream. I got henna painted on my hands in the courtyard. But halfway through, I rushed to the bathroom again.

Patrick found me hunched over the sink, tears in my eyes. He didn't ask questions. Just handed me a cool towel.

Later that night, curled up in bed, I finally spoke the fear.

"I thought being on the pill meant we didn't have to think about this."

He pulled me close. "Time zones, schedules… maybe it threw things off."

"So what do we do now?"

He kissed my forehead. "If it's meant to be… maybe it is."

Rishikesh gave us peace. We checked into a yoga retreat near the Ganges. The early mornings, the chanting, the calm—it was everything I hadn't known I needed. I joined a gentle yoga class, but left halfway through when the nausea hit again. Patrick was waiting near the river, warm tea in hand.

"You okay?"

I leaned into him. "Just tired. Of this. Of not knowing."

He didn't try to fix it. He just held me. "You don't need to know everything right now. Just let your body talk. I'm listening."

In Pokhara, Nepal, the air was cooler. The lake glistened under wide skies, and the mountains in the distance felt like protectors. We hiked through the Annapurna foothills—I, slower than usual. Patrick never left my side.

One morning, I barely made it to the bathroom in time. The dry retching was loud and painful. Patrick came in, quiet, calm. He knelt beside me, pulling strands of hair off my sweaty face.

"Well," he said with a soft smile, brushing the sticky strands back, "maybe it really was meant to be."

I looked up at him, exhausted but warm inside. "Maybe it was."

We still didn't know. But every morning, my stomach turned. Every day, nausea came in waves. And every time my head met a toilet bowl or a side curb, Patrick was there, holding my hair and whispering gentle things.

That night in Pokhara, we sat under a candlelit lantern at a rooftop cafe. The stars blinked above the mountains. I reached for his hand.

"I don't know what's coming next," I said, "but I know I don't want to do it without you."

He squeezed my hand. "You never have to."

I stared at the calendar app on my phone. Counting. Again.

And no matter how many times I counted, I got the same answer. I'm definitely late.

I pressed a hand to my belly. I'd told myself the stress, the flights, the change in time zones—those were the reasons.

But maybe they weren't.

My reflection blinked back at me from the bathroom mirror, pale and wide-eyed.

And for once, I didn't look away.

By the time we touched down in Kyoto, the nausea had become a permanent passenger on this journey. But Patrick never wavered—his hand always ready, his eyes constantly checking mine, as if silently asking, how are you really feeling, Lucy?

Kyoto was peaceful, a city that seemed to whisper rather than shout. We wandered through ancient temples, their wooden beams soaked in centuries of incense and quiet reverence. I closed my eyes under the bright red arches of Fushimi Inari Shrine and imagined asking the gods for strength, not just for me, but for us.

One morning, we found a quiet tea-house tucked into the hills near a bamboo grove. We sat cross-legged on tatami mats while an elderly woman led us through a traditional tea ceremony. As I sipped the warm, earthy matcha, I could feel my stomach settle for the first time in days.

Patrick leaned close, whispering, "Maybe we should just drink tea for the rest of the trip."

I smiled weakly. "Only if you promise to keep holding my hair when it doesn't sit well."

He kissed my cheek. "Deal."

From Kyoto, we sped into the electric heartbeat of Tokyo. The city pulsed with light and energy, every street a different universe. We ate ramen in a standing-only bar down a narrow alley, and I watched Patrick devour three bowls like he hadn't eaten in weeks.

"I think the baby's hungry," he joked, rubbing my stomach gently even though we still weren't sure if there was a baby at all.

I swatted his hand away playfully. "You mean you're hungry." But something about the way he looked at me—tender, hopeful—made my chest tighten in the best way.

As we passed a coffee stall, the sharp scent of roasted beans hit my nose. I gagged instantly.

"But you love coffee," Patrick said.

"I used to," I said, pressing the back of my hand to my mouth.

He didn't say anything, but I felt his eyes on me the rest of the day.

We stayed one night in a capsule hotel, just for the experience. We ended up ditching our own pods halfway through the night and squeezing into one together, giggling like teenagers trying not to get caught. Wrapped in each other, I forgot for a little while that my body didn't quite feel like my own lately.

By the time we reached Busan, South Korea, the chill of the coastal breeze was a relief. We wandered seafood markets, laughing at the live octopus squirming in shallow tanks. Patrick dared me to try one, but the smell alone sent me running to the nearest bin.

He didn't say a word. Just followed me, hair tie in hand, and gently pulled my hair back like he always did.

"Maybe we should stick to cooked food," he offered once I

resurfaced, breathless and pale.

"Or just ice," I muttered. "Ice seems safe."

We arrived in Seoul a few days later, and despite the nausea and exhaustion, I fell in love with the city instantly. It had a rhythm—fast but not frantic, vibrant yet warm. We explored royal palaces where guards in traditional hanbok stood as still as statues, and we ate tteokbokki and hotteok from street vendors that lined bustling alleys glowing with neon signs.

One night, we hiked to Namsan Tower. Patrick said he wanted to see the city from above, and we stood side by side, looking out over a million blinking lights.

He slipped a small lock from his pocket—one he'd bought without telling me.

"Write your name next to mine," he said, offering me a marker.

"Isn't this something couples do when they're... like... forever?" I asked.

Patrick turned to me, eyes soft. "Aren't we?"

I stared at him, the marker suddenly heavy in my hand. I didn't answer with words. I just wrote our names on the lock, snapped it shut on the fence, and kissed him like he was already mine forever.

As we walked back down the hill, the cool wind brushing our cheeks, Patrick laced his fingers through mine. "You still feeling sick?" he asked quietly.

I nodded. "Yeah. But it's getting easier."

And with every step we took, I started to believe it was true. That night in Seoul, something shifted.

Maybe it was the view from Namsan Tower, or the lock with our names now nestled among thousands of others, but something about that moment made everything feel… more real. He wasn't just the guy I was traveling with. He was the one I wanted to wake up next to every morning—nausea, chaos, and all.

We returned to our hotel late, the room glowing softly from the city lights sneaking through the curtains. I sat at the edge of the bed, slipping off my shoes.

Patrick came up behind me and gently brushed my hair over one shoulder.

His fingers grazed the curve of my neck, lingering just long enough to send a ripple through me.

"You've been so strong through all of this, Lucy," he said quietly.

I turned toward him, my breath already uneven. "I don't feel strong."

"You don't need to," he murmured. "Just let me take care of you tonight."

He kissed me—not rushed or eager, but slow, like he was trying to sink into me without ever letting go. His hands slid beneath my shirt and lifted it over my head, fingertips skimming my skin as if memorising the texture of my resilience.

His mouth followed the trail, kissing along my collarbone, down the slope of my breast, while I peeled away the fabric between us until we were bare skin against skin, warm and vulnerable under the soft Seoul moonlight.

He guided me onto the bed, but this time he didn't hover or pause. He came down on top of me, every inch of him flush with mine, the weight of him grounding me in the present.

His voice was low. "Tell me if anything doesn't feel right."

"Everything about this feels right," I whispered, wrapping my arms around his back.

He moved inside me with a slowness that wasn't caution. A kind of trust that didn't need words. He moved with patience, depth, and a tenderness that almost undid me.

We breathed in sync, eyes locked, our rhythm unhurried— each stroke a conversation of its own. No frantic pace. No rushing toward release. Just this: closeness, tension, the build of something real curling tighter with each thrust.

My body pulsed around him, and the deeper he went, the more I came undone—not with moans or shouts, but soft gasps, my nails pressing lightly into his back, my lips brushing against his temple.

He shifted slightly, angling deeper, and I cried out before I could stop it, not from pain, but from the sudden, perfect pleasure that made the world vanish.

Patrick groaned, his forehead pressed to mine, his thrusts growing sharper, faster, until the edge between us crumbled completely.

I reached for him as I came, limbs tightening, body trembling around his. He followed a breath later, shuddering inside me, his hand clutching mine like he needed an anchor.

We stayed like that—bodies tangled, still joined, our breathing slowly falling into rhythm with the city pulsing softly beyond the curtains.

He didn't speak. He just kissed my shoulder and pulled me closer.

And this time, I didn't think about tomorrow. Or tests. Or what came next.

Just him. Me. And the way everything in that moment felt

exactly right.

I traced lazy circles on Patrick's chest. "Where do you see yourself in five years?"

He chuckled. "Is this a job interview?"

"I'm serious."

He paused. "Honestly? I don't see a place. I see a person. You. Maybe a dog that barks too much. Maybe… a family."

I swallowed. "You see all that with me?"

"I already do."

And in that moment, I wasn't sure if the flutter in my stomach was nerves or something else entirely.

As we drifted to sleep in that Seoul hotel, the city glowing outside our window and our hearts wrapped up in something neither of us could name yet, I realised…

Whatever came next—sickness, love, even the possibility of a baby—I wasn't afraid.

 Because he was here.

And so was I. And this?

This was a moment we'd never forget.

Chapter 15

The Final Stretch

We arrived in Ubud, Bali, to the scent of incense and rain-soaked jungle. It was the kind of place that whispered instead of spoke — all rice terraces, temple offerings, and the constant hum of life hidden among the green.

Our villa overlooked the lush hills, and mornings began with birdsong and the distant gurgle of river water. We swung over jungle canopies, explored the monkey forest (where one particularly bold monkey tried to steal Patrick's sunglasses), and got caught in a downpour halfway through a temple walk. Instead of running, we danced in the rain.

But even paradise couldn't distract me from the queasiness that had taken up permanent residence in my stomach. Every morning, I'd wake up, sprint to the bathroom, and spend the first part of the day dry-heaving while Patrick held back my hair like it was second nature.

"I think this baby really likes Bali," he said one morning, handing me a cool washcloth.

"We don't even know if it's a baby," I said between deep breaths.

He knelt beside me, brushing sweat-damp strands from my

face. "Then it's a very dramatic stomach bug with excellent timing."

We both laughed. We still hadn't taken a test — partly because we hadn't found one in English, and partly because I wasn't sure I was ready to know for sure. This trip was about discovering the world. And somewhere along the way, we'd started discovering a life. Patrick convinced me to visit a local healer.

It's a mix of awkward, emotional, and spiritual. The healer places her hands on Lucy's belly and smiles knowingly. "Your energy is not alone." Lucy doesn't know if she believes in it, but it sticks with her.

In Seminyak, we shifted gears. Beachfront sunsets, poolside cocktails (well, mocktails for me), and spa days. Patrick booked us a couple's massage, which would've been relaxing if the smell of the oils hadn't triggered another round of vomiting mid-session. He held my hand while I apologised profusely to the horrified masseuse.

"I think you've officially christened every bathroom on this island," he teased later, rubbing my back as I curled up in a fluffy white robe.

"Add that to the list of things I never expected from this trip," I groaned.

Later that afternoon, Patrick disappeared for a little while. I thought he'd gone to grab a drink or check in on something with reception, but instead, he returned with a wide grin and a folded-up blanket under one arm.

"Put on something comfy," he said, "and come with me."

I followed him barefoot down the narrow path that led past the pool and out to the sand, where the sun was beginning to dip low over the water. There, spread out on the beach, was a little setup— soft towels, a basket full of snacks, and two chilled coconuts waiting like they belonged in a travel magazine.

"You brought a picnic?" I said, smiling.

"Not just any picnic," he said, handing me a drink. "Mocktail magic. I asked the bar to make you a coconut-lime fizz with ginger, supposedly good for nausea—and very Instagrammable."

I laughed, curling up beside him on the blanket. "You're ridiculous."

"I'm thoughtful," he corrected, clinking his coconut against mine. "And maybe a little ridiculous."

We sat there in comfortable silence, sipping our drinks and watching the waves curl and crash in slow rhythm.

"This is perfect," I whispered.

"I know," he said. "That's why I planned it."

As the sun dipped low and cast gold across the ocean, we sat in silence on the sand.

I leaned into him, resting my head on his shoulder. He smelled like sunscreen and salt and safety.

"**I love you**," he said suddenly. No buildup, no hesitation. My breath caught. I turned to him, blinking.

"You… what?"

"I love you, Lucy," he said again, his voice steady. "I think I've loved you since the moment you opened your front door and made that cheeky joke about the stairs. I just didn't know it yet."

I laughed, eyes stinging. "I love you, too. Even if you make fun of me during my most glamorous moments."

We kissed under the Bali sky, and just like that, the words that had lived between us for weeks were finally out loud.

That night, back at our villa, the rain began to fall—soft and steady, like a lullaby for the jungle.

Patrick lit the candles on the bedside table without saying a word. The glow danced across the walls, golden and warm, and I watched him move through the space like he already knew every part of me. Maybe he did.

I stood at the doorway, the ocean breeze still clinging to my skin, and when he looked at me, just looked—my knees went weak.

"Come here," he said softly.

I walked to him slowly, heart thudding, breath shaky. His hands slid around my waist and pulled me in. He kissed me gently at first—tender, unhurried—then deeper, fuller, like he was pouring everything he felt into it.

His fingers slipped under my dress and found the hem, lifting it slowly over my head. It pooled at my feet as his eyes swept over me, pausing at the slight curve of my stomach. "Still not sure," I whispered, self-conscious. "Still maybe." He rested a hand there, warm and steady. "Maybe it's enough."

I didn't cry. But I almost did.

He undressed without rushing, each movement deliberate, and when we were both bare, he led me to the bed. The sheets were cool beneath us, but his body was all heat.

He hovered over me, brushing a strand of hair behind my ear. "Tell me if anything hurts."

"It won't," I said. "Not with you." And it didn't.

He entered me slowly, inch by inch, stretching me open with a pressure that made me gasp—but not from pain. From the unbearable rightness of it. Like my body had been waiting for this shape. This man. His eyes never leaving mine. The rhythm he set was unhurried, as if we had forever. His hands roamed my body like he was relearning every inch—gentle over my hips, firm at my waist, and worshipful at my chest.

I arched into him, meeting every thrust with soft gasps, the sound of rain outside keeping time with the beat of our bodies.

"I love you," he whispered again, right into my mouth.

I pulled him closer, wrapping my legs around his waist,

wanting all of him—his strength, his softness, his certainty when everything in me felt like maybe.

When I came, it was quiet—just a soft whimper, my body trembling beneath him. And when he followed, burying his face in my neck, I held him like I could anchor him there forever.

Afterwards, we lay tangled together, the candlelight flickering low. His hand rested lightly on my stomach.

"Even if it's not a baby," he said, "it's something that brought us here."

I nodded, barely able to speak.

Outside, the rain kept falling. Inside, it was just us.

In Nusa Penida, we found hidden beaches with turquoise water and sheer cliffs that made my knees wobble. We snorkelled through coral gardens and held hands as we floated side by side in the sea. I was still sick every morning, still tired all the time, but Patrick made it feel less like a burden and more like… something sacred.

We hiked down to Kelingking Beach. It was harder than I expected—sharp stone steps carved into a narrow ridge, with no railings and just open sky on either side. Halfway down, I froze.

I looked down at the turquoise sea far below and felt something twist in my stomach that had nothing to do with morning sickness.

"Patrick," I whispered.

He turned instantly, climbing back up a few steps to where I stood.

"I can't," I said, voice shaking. "It's too high. I feel like I'm going to fall."

He didn't laugh. Didn't tease. He just took my hand in his, threading our fingers together.

"We don't have to go all the way," he said gently. "Just one step at a time. I've got you."

With him beside me, I took a deep breath and moved forward, one careful step at a time. We didn't make it all the way to the bottom. But we made it far enough to see the beach spread below us like a secret.

And in that moment, I realised it wasn't just the drop I was afraid of. It was everything I couldn't control—my body, the possibility of a baby, the fact that I was falling… fast.

Patrick squeezed my hand like he knew. Like he'd already caught me.

That night, after a slow dinner of grilled fish and coconut rice, we lay side by side on a deck chair, a light breeze brushing over our skin. The stars blinked above us, bold and endless.

"What would we even name a baby if there is one?" Patrick asked suddenly.

I laughed. "We haven't even taken a test."

"True. But if there is something growing in there…" He reached over and gently rested a hand on my belly. "It deserves a cool name, don't you think?"

"Oh, so you're aiming for cool now?" I teased.

"Well, yeah. Something like… Nova. Or Atlas."

I raised an eyebrow. "Those are names for a star and a Greek god."

"Exactly. Epic."

I shook my head, smiling. "You're ridiculous."

"You love it," he said, grinning.

And maybe I did. I didn't say anything. I just reached over, took his hand in mine, and rested it back on my stomach.

We lay there under the stars, not needing to know what came next.

Just existing in the maybe. Together.

As we laid that night, tangled in white sheets."You're growing something inside you," "Whether it's a baby or not… It's something real."

Our final stop was Sidemen — a quiet village carved into the hills. No Wi-Fi, no distractions. Just time. We sat on our porch wrapped in blankets, sipping warm tea as the wind whispered through the trees.

"This place feels like the end of something," I said.

He looked at me, brushing his thumb across my knuckles. "Or the beginning."

We spent those last days talking about home — about what it would mean to go back. About the letter from my parents, and everything they gave me. About the possibility that I might be pregnant, and what that would change.

But we didn't make plans. Not yet.

Instead, we watched the sun rise over the mountains and promised each other one thing:

No matter what the test says, or where life takes us next, this?

This will always be a moment we'll never forget.

Chapter 16

The 1% Becomes Everything

The plane landed with a gentle thud, wheels screeching as we touched down on home soil. My phone **buzzed** the second we were allowed to switch it on. I sent a quick message to Sienna:

"I'm back. Come to mine for lunch?"

The moment I hit send, my nerves kicked in. Not because of seeing Sienna, but because of what I was about to do next.

We stopped at the doctor's office on the way home. Dr. Marla had been my GP since I was a baby, and as soon as her office door opened, I was greeted by her familiar warm smile.

"Lucy! You're back! How was the trip? You look… tired," she said, studying my face.

Without thinking, I blurted it out. "Well, maybe it's the time zone difference… or maybe it's because I'm 99% sure I'm pregnant."

Patrick shifted beside me, and Dr. Marla raised a brow. "Ninety-nine percent?"

I nodded. "Yeah. We've been travelling for the last six months. I was on the pill but totally forgot to adjust it for all the time zone changes. Halfway through the trip, I started getting sick every morning. Constant nausea. My belly feels like it's growing, but that could also be the global buffet I've been enjoying."

Patrick laughed. So did Dr. Marla.

"Alright then," she said kindly. "Climb up. Let's have a look."

I lay down on the exam bed while she pulled the ultrasound machine over. The cold gel hit my skin with a jolt. Patrick stood beside me, squeezing my hand.

Black and white shapes blurred across the screen. I squinted, trying to make sense of it all.

"Glad you know what you're looking at," I said. "Because to me, it just looks like a snowstorm."

Dr. Marla smiled. "Look here. See that little flicker? That's the heartbeat. And that—that's your baby."

My breath hitched.

Baby.

Until that moment, there had always been a 1% chance I was wrong that this was just a long bout of travel sickness or stress.

Patrick must have seen the panic on my face. He leaned in, pressing a kiss to my temple.

"It's okay," he whispered. "It was obviously meant to be."

Dr. Marla took some measurements. "You're about thirteen

weeks along," she confirmed, handing me a small printed photo of the scan.

I didn't know I was holding my breath until I heard it—**thump-thump-thump.** So tiny. So real. Tears burned the corners of my eyes before I could stop them.

I stared at the grainy image in disbelief. A little grainy photo. A flicker of light. And somehow, everything had changed. "Congratulations, both of you."

Patrick stepped out into the hallway and I found him back against the wall, staring at the ultrasound photo.

"You okay?" I asked.

"I will be," he said, voice thick. "I'm just trying to wrap my head around the fact that I'm going to be someone's dad."

The drive home was quiet. Emotions swirled between us like fog on a rainy day—excitement, fear, disbelief. We pulled into the driveway and retrieved our bags, wordless.

The moment we walked back into the house, it hit me—we're not just unpacking suitcases today. We're unpacking a whole new future.

I stood in the doorway of the living room, staring at the framed photo of Mum and Dad on the sideboard. The same house. Same walls. But everything felt different now. Like we'd stepped into someone else's life—and yet, it was mine.

I drop my bags, and Patrick does the same. He steps forward and pulls me into his arms, his hands warm on my back, his voice low and steady.

"It's going to be okay," he whispers. "We've got this."

I nod against his chest, swallowing back the swirl of emotions—shock, nerves, joy, panic. Then I remember something else: lunch with Sienna.

I slip out of Patrick's arms and text her:

"Still on for lunch?"

A second later, her reply pings: *"Be there soon."*

Fifteen minutes later, I hear the door open and her familiar voice ring out.

"Lucy?"

"In the kitchen!" I call.

She walks in, stylish as ever, sunglasses still perched on her head. But her eyes narrow as she looks me over, top to toe, then back up again.

"You've got news," she says flatly. "I can feel it."

I don't answer. I just stare at her, emotions too big to shape into words.

She tilts her head. "Oh my god. You're pregnant, aren't

you?" I blink, stunned by how fast she clocked it.

She tilts her head, crosses her arms, and smirks.

"He knocked you up, didn't he? Fucked you so good your body couldn't help but get pregnant."

I burst out laughing. Loudly. Too loudly.

Right on cue, Patrick walks in from the hallway, mid-smirk and holding a glass of water.

Sienna's gaze shifts, taking him in for the first time. Her jaw drops.

"God damn," she says, eyes wide. "Even better in person." I can't stop laughing.

Patrick lifts a brow. "I'm going to assume you're Sienna."

She shrugs unapologetically. "You must be the reason she's glowing... and gagging every morning."

Still chuckling, I reach for the black-and-white ultrasound photo from the counter and hand it to her.

"Well, Sienna... looks like you're going to be an aunt."

She stares at the image, then at me. Her eyes mist over for half a second before she playfully shoves my shoulder.

"Shit. You're really doing it, huh?"

"I guess I am," I say softly, looking at Patrick, who's now

standing beside me, his arm around my waist.

"You remember that time we played mums and babies when we were kids?" she said, wiping under one eye. "You always wanted twins. Guess one's a start."

Sienna pulls out her phone and says, "I need wine… wait, no. You can't. Dammit."

Patrick laughs, then nudges me. "Think it's time?"

I nod. We've been sitting on it long enough. He picks up his phone. I grab mine.

Together, we upload the same photo—the ultrasound picture, grainy and perfect.

Caption:

When you take an around-the-world adventure… fall in love with the love of your life… and create a new life.

When two becomes three.

Within seconds, the likes and comments start flooding in.

Patrick set his phone down, his arm still looped around my waist. I kept mine in hand, watching as the comments began flooding in within seconds of the post going live.

Sienna leaned over my shoulder. "Let me see!"

We all huddled together around my screen as the likes

stacked up fast and the messages rolled in.

"Omg! Congratulations, you two!!"

"No way! This is the sweetest news I've seen all week." "You're going to be the most stunning mum, Lucy." "Wait... WHAT? I need the full story asap!"

Sienna snorted. "You're breaking the internet. I'm pretty sure someone just tagged their Grandma in it."

Patrick laughed. "I mean... it *is* pretty shareable content. Love story, unexpected pregnancy, glowing girlfriend, hot boyfriend—what's not to like?"

Sienna raised a brow. "Humble much?"

He grinned. "Just stating facts."

I scrolled further and saw a name I hadn't seen in years. *Mrs. K*—our old primary school teacher.

"Your parents would be so proud, Lucy. They'd be smiling down on you both. Love always, Mrs. K."

I blinked hard, swallowing the sudden emotion rising in my chest. My voice caught. "She used to garden with Mum."

Sienna gently placed her hand on mine.

Patrick kissed my temple. I leaned into him, trying not to let the tears fall—not yet.

Then Sienna suddenly gasped and spun toward me.

"Wait—hold up. If you're having a baby... I get to throw the baby shower, right? Like, that's non-negotiable."

Patrick chuckled. "We haven't even figured out the nursery and you're already on decorations?"

"Oh, babe," Sienna waved him off, "I've *already* got themes. Plural. I've got a whole Pinterest board for this exact moment."

"You *have* a baby shower Pinterest board?" I asked, laughing through a sniffle.

"You think I wasn't manifesting this? Please—I started planning your baby shower the second you two ditched the condoms, relied on the pill across twelve time zones, and started sexing your way around the world like it was your full-time job."

Patrick choked on his water. "Wow, Sienna."

His face turned a shade of red I'd never seen before. He looked at me, eyes wide with mock betrayal. "Is *this* what you two talk about when I'm not around? My... global performance record?"

I doubled over with laughter, clutching my stomach. "She's not wrong."

He groaned, dragging a hand over his face. "Great. My sex life's now an international headline."

Sienna just grinned, totally unfazed. "Oh, honey, it's been front-page news since Rome."

We all laughed, and in that moment—with love pouring in from phones, with Patrick's arm around me and Sienna planning a party that didn't exist yet—I realised something I hadn't dared to admit until now.

We weren't alone in this.

We were surrounded by people who cared, who wanted to celebrate this new life with us.

And maybe… just maybe… I was ready to celebrate it too.

And for the first time in a while, I don't feel scared about what's next. I feel ready. We're ready.

Chapter 17

The Calm Before The Storm

Lunch was easy, filled with laughter and familiar comfort.

"Alright," Sienna said, "I need every juicy detail. All of them. Don't hold back."

Patrick glanced at me, raising a brow. "Should I leave the room for this?"

Sienna grinned. "Probably, unless you want to hear us dissect your sexual performance in graphic detail."

Patrick smirked, kissed my cheek, and whispered, "I'll leave you ladies to it. Try not to exaggerate too much."

He disappeared upstairs, and I turned back to Sienna, who was already cracking open a bottle of wine I wasn't going to drink.

"So," she said, leaning forward like we were trading secrets in high school again, "was it good?"

I laughed, already blushing. "It was… more than good. It was like every part of my body finally understood what it was made for. He's gentle but knows exactly what he's doing. And he doesn't rush. Like, he takes his time—every single time. It's like he's memorising me."

"Damn," Sienna whispered, her voice low and wicked. "So, like… shower sex? Couch sex? Against-the-wall sex?"

"All of the above," I groaned, covering my face with both hands, the heat rushing up my neck.

Sienna let out a high-pitched, delighted laugh. "That's my girl! You went and found yourself your very own Eiffel Tower—with better lighting and no wait time."

I peeked between my fingers and laughed. "He's like a walking sex dream, and somehow… he's real."

She leaned in, eyes dancing. "Okay, seriously—why didn't you warn me? I thought sex was just moaning, a bit of heavy breathing, and hoping you remembered to shave. But this?" She exhaled like she was reliving it with me. "It sounds like he didn't just touch your body—he possessed it. Like he was reading a map made only for his hands and mouth."

I bit my lip, my voice dropping. "It felt like he was devouring me with his eyes before he even laid a finger on me. And once he did—God. Every touch was slow and purposeful, like I was something to be studied, unwrapped, worshipped. He didn't rush. Not once. He took his time like he had forever."

Sienna's gaze narrowed, laser-focused. "You're glowing. Like, post-orgasm, wrecked-for-days kind of glowing."

I laughed, but my voice softened. "It wasn't just the sex, though, trust me, that nearly tore me open in the best way. It's how he touches me. Like I'm the storm and the eye of it, like his hands are both reverent and greedy. But the real killer?"

She raised a brow. "There's more?"

"It's afterwards," I whispered, my throat tightening. "When we're tangled up, breathless, my body still humming… It's the way he looks at me. Like I'm not just something he wants, but something he needs. Like I'm his beginning and end."

Sienna blinked slowly, visibly moved. "Shit, Luce."

"He memorises me. Not just my body, but the way I feel afterwards. Like he's pressing all my pieces into his own skin just so he won't forget."

Sienna let out a long breath, her voice hushed. "Damn. That's not just good sex. That's the kind that fucks with your soul. The kind that changes how you walk through the world."

She reached for my hand, squeezed it gently. "You deserve that. You deserve every second of that magic."

We chatted for another hour—about the trip, the food, the temples, the beaches. Sienna beamed the whole time, genuinely happy for me. I told her there were so many memories, so many moments I'll never forget.

As the sun began to dip low behind the trees, Sienna gathered her things. She kissed my cheek and rubbed my stomach playfully. "Take care of that little world traveller, okay?"

"I will."

She left, and I wandered upstairs. Patrick was in the shower, steam curling beneath the bathroom door. I stood by the window, watching the last sliver of light fade behind the trees, my hand resting over the curve of my belly.

I was smiling, thinking about the future, about Patrick, about our baby and the life we were building—when something shifted.

Movement.

In the shadows at the edge of the property. I froze. My gaze sharpened. There, across the street. A figure. Tall. Familiar. My heart skipped a beat. No. It couldn't be.

I didn't move from the window. Just slowly reached for the blinds and tugged them closed with a soft click. Then—**buzz**.

My phone lit up on the table. One new message from Zeke.

I see you.

My hand froze over my belly. A chill ran down my spine and a scream ripped from my throat—loud, sharp, primal. The phone slipped from my hands, crashing to the floor. Patrick burst out of the bathroom, still dripping wet, soap suds clinging to his chest, not even bothering to grab a towel. He froze when he saw my face. Terror. Real, bone-deep terror. His eyes dropped to the phone on the floor. He scooped it up, read the message, and went still. Then his jaw clenched. Without a word, he yanked on a pair of damp shorts and bolted downstairs, rage radiating off him like heat.

"Patrick!" I shouted, racing after him, my heart hammering. But before either of us could even touch the door handle, Zeke was already there. On the front step. Smirking.

Patrick flung the door open so hard it cracked against the wall. "What the fuck are you doing here?"

Zeke's eyes didn't leave mine. "What the hell were you thinking, Lucy? Throwing everything away for him? Carrying his kid like some cheap replacement?

Patrick didn't give him another second. His fist exploded across Zeke's jaw with a sickening crack, sending him sprawling into the garden bed like a broken toy.

"Leave. Now. Don't come back."

Zeke staggered, holding his jaw, glaring at us both. "You'll regret this."

Patrick took a step forward.

Zeke backed off. Then turned. And walked away.

Patrick slammed the door shut, locking it with shaking hands. He turned to me, chest heaving, water still dripping from his hair.

I was trembling. He crossed the room in two strides and pulled me into his arms. Wrapped me up so tightly I could barely breathe—but I didn't want to.

"I've got you," he murmured, voice steady but low with fury. "He won't hurt you. Not ever again."

And somehow, despite the fear still sitting in my chest like a weight, I believed him.

Chapter 18

The Quiet Collapse

Patrick

The house was quiet, but my mind wasn't.

Lucy had fallen asleep curled on her side, one hand resting over the soft curve of her belly, her breath a slow rhythm that used to calm me. Not tonight.

I sat in the dark for what felt like hours, listening, like I was waiting for something. A noise. A knock. Another threat. But nothing came.

Eventually, I slid out of bed, careful not to wake her, and walked down the hallway. My legs moved on their own, like they knew where I needed to be. The bathroom mirror greeted me with a stranger's face. Hair still damp from the shower, jaw tight, shoulders hunched like I was waiting for a fight that hadn't finished. My eyes were bloodshot. Hollow. I splashed cold water on my face. Once. Twice. It didn't help. I braced both hands against the sink and stared into the glass. My reflection didn't blink. All night, I'd been pretending I was okay. But the truth was, Zeke showing up didn't just piss me off. It cracked something open. I slid down the wall, landing hard on the tiles, and dragged a hand through my hair. My lungs felt too tight. My chest was too full. My thoughts were too loud. I could've lost her. That's all I could think. Over and over.

What if I hadn't been home? What if he'd gotten to her before I had? What if she'd been alone and scared, and I hadn't been there?

A tremble ran through my hands. And beneath all that fear… was something else. Something I hadn't wanted to name. I don't know how to do this. I never had a father to show me what being a man looked like— not really. Not the kind of man Lucy needs. And Mum? She was the closest thing I had to feeling safe. Her arms, her voice… they made the world feel smaller, softer. But they were both gone now.

Cancer took Mum fast. And Dad? Grief took him even faster. One day, he just… stopped showing up. His body stayed, but he didn't. I didn't get a guidebook. I didn't get the blueprint for how to build a family, how to protect one. And now here I was—a father. Or I would be, if I didn't screw it up first. The fear hit me like a sucker punch.

What if I can't protect them? What if I fail her? Or worse… what if this beautiful, chaotic, wild thing we've built falls apart, and I'm the one who lets it? A sharp breath rattled out of me. A sob. - Shaky, quiet, guttural. I pressed my palms to my eyes and let the silence eat me alive. I didn't know how long I sat there, staring into nothing. The silence wrapped around me like a vice, tight, relentless, until warmth touched me. A presence. Her. But then—warmth.

I didn't hear her footsteps. I didn't need to. The moment her warmth reached me, I knew it was her. Like my body always knew when she was near.

Lucy sat beside me, barefoot in an oversized tee, and reached for my hand. No questions. No words. Just her fingers threading through mine like she'd always known I'd fall apart one day—and that she'd be the one to put me back together.

"I'm scared," I said, voice cracking. "Not of him. Of… messing this up. Of not being enough. Of not knowing how to do this without them."

Lucy didn't tell me I was wrong. She didn't say I was enough. She just leaned her head against my shoulder.

"You're already doing it," she whispered. "You're here. You showed up. And you're staying. That's more than most."

I pulled her into my lap, burying my face into the curve of her neck, breathing her in like she was air. Her belly pressed between us—our baby, our future—and something about it grounded me. I held her like she was all I had. Because she was. And maybe I didn't have a guidebook. But I had this. Her. Us. A reason to stay soft and strong in equal measure. A reason to fight harder than I ever have.

I kissed her temple and whispered, "I'll protect you both. With everything I've got. I don't care if I have to rip the sky in half to do it." And in the stillness that followed, I knew something for sure:

I wasn't just scared anymore.

I was ready.

Ready to be the kind of man my father never figured out how to be.

Ready to be the kind of father I never had.

Because loving Lucy wasn't just something I felt. It was who I'd become, who I'd keep choosing—every day, every breath, for the rest of my life.

Chapter 19

Their Room, Our Future

The next morning, the air felt different. Calmer.

The light through the kitchen window stretched across the floor in golden ribbons. The scent of Earl Grey and coffee swirled in the air, and toast popped from the toaster with a soft click. We weren't saying much, but the silence wasn't empty— it was full of something tender and warm, like the quiet moments you don't want to disturb with words.

Patrick placed his mug in the sink, turned to me, and said simply, "I don't want to go back to my place."

I looked up from my tea.

"I mean," he continued, "I know we sort of already live together... we just spent six months sharing hotel rooms and jungle hammocks." He said, tracing his finger along the rim of his coffee mug.

"But it's different waking up next to you here. It feels like... home. Like, I don't want to leave, not even for a second, so if you're okay with it, I'd like to make it official. Move in. Fully."

The words hit me in a way I didn't expect. Warmth bloomed in my chest. A tear threatened to sneak out, but I blinked it back and smiled.

"Are you sure you want to live with a pregnant, hormonal, maybe-slightly-unhinged woman?"

Patrick stepped closer and pressed a kiss to my forehead. "Absolutely. But I want to keep my job too. I want to contribute— to show up for you in every way I can. Even if that means coming home late sometimes, buried in spreadsheets."

I laughed softly. "You and your numbers. That's fair."

He ran his hands along my arms. "So… do I need a key? Or do I just never leave?"

"Never leave," I whispered. "But I'll get you a key anyway." Later, we curled up on the couch, sorting through mail and talking about what came next—doctor appointments, cravings, names we liked and didn't. Somewhere in the lull of our conversation, I looked up and said, "I think I'm going to hire the house staff back."

Patrick blinked. "Wait—what staff?"

I sighed. "Before Mum and Dad passed, we had help. A housekeeper, a gardener, who came a couple of times a week. They were practically part of the family. But when they died… I couldn't face anyone in this house. I let them all go."

"You needed time," he said gently.

"I get that."

"Yeah. But now? I don't want this place to feel empty anymore."

He squeezed my hand. "Then let's fill it."

We wandered through the house that afternoon—the kind of slow steps you take when imagining something new. When we reached the door to Dad's old office, we paused. Neither of us had been in there since the day we packed up his boxes and found the folder—the one that changed everything.

I turned to Patrick, something thoughtful in my voice.

"This was Dad's office. The one where we found the travel folder. I haven't opened it since that day."

Patrick placed his hand gently on the doorknob. "You want to go in?"

I nodded.

He opened the door, and we stepped inside. The air was still, full of dust and memories. The desk sat just as we'd left it. Shelves were still lined with old books. The soft light pouring through the window gave the room a quiet peace.

"I was thinking…" I began slowly, "maybe this could be your office now. So you can work from home when you need to. It feels like the right space. And I think Dad would've liked that."

Patrick glanced around, visibly moved. "Are you sure?"

"Yeah," I said. "He'd be happy someone was using it again."

We lingered in silence for a few heartbeats. Then we crossed the hall and stopped outside the door to my parents' bedroom.

"This," I said, "could be the nursery."

Patrick hesitated. "Their room?"

I nodded, emotion rising in my chest.

"It's close to ours. It's filled with love. And maybe… maybe they can keep watching over the baby this way."

His smile was soft as he pulled me into a hug. "Then it's perfect." His hand found the doorknob. "You sure?"

I drew in a steadying breath. "Yeah. I think I'm ready."

He turned the handle, and the door creaked softly as it opened. We stepped inside. The air smelled faintly of Mum's perfume. The bed was still perfectly made, the way she always kept it. The room hadn't changed—as if it had been waiting. For this moment, maybe.

Patrick slipped his arm around me, and I leaned my head on his shoulder.

"It still feels like them," I whispered. "But it doesn't feel heavy. It feels… comforting. Like they're giving us their blessing."

We stood there for a while, just breathing it in. No rush. No pressure. Just quiet understanding between us.

Patrick walked toward the wardrobe and gently opened the door. Hanging inside, untouched since the day Mum last wore it, was her favourite scarf—a soft cream with delicate embroidery along the edges. I reached for it, fingers trembling slightly.

"She wore this all the time," I said softly. "It still smells like her."

Patrick took it from the hanger and stepped closer, draping

it gently around my shoulders.

"She'd love knowing it's still keeping someone she loves warm," he said.

Tears welled in my eyes, but they didn't fall. Instead, I smiled, wrapping the scarf tighter around me.

I remembered Mum wrapping it around my neck on chilly mornings, tucking the ends in with a smile that said she'd always take care of me. I thought it would hurt more. To imagine repainting the walls, tucking baby blankets into drawers where Mum once folded her scarves. But instead of feeling like I was erasing them, it felt like layering love, past over future, future over past. And as the late afternoon light poured into the room, I realised that some doors don't just close on the past—they open to the future. Patrick gently closed the wardrobe doors, dust still dancing in the sunlight.

"I want Sienna here tomorrow when we start packing it up," I said. "She should be part of this. She's always been by my side."

Patrick nodded, surprised but pleased. "Of course. She should be here for this."

I nodded slowly, heart full.

"I just messaged her," I said, holding up my phone so he could read the screen. *"We're packing up their room tomorrow. Turning it into the nursery."*

Almost instantly, my phone lit up with her reply.

"I'll hold your hand every step of the way. We'll do it

together. Just like everything else."

Tears pricked at the corners of my eyes, but I smiled. With Patrick and Sienna by my side, I knew everything would be okay.

I felt ready.

Chapter 20

One Box At A Time

Sienna arrived just after 9 a.m., a reusable coffee cup in one hand and a determined look on her face.

Patrick opened the front door before I could even reach it. He smiled at her, genuinely warm. "Hey. Thanks for coming. I know Lucy's really grateful… and so am I. She's stronger with you around."

Sienna gave him a wink. "Of course she is. I'm her emotional support tornado." She stepped inside and pulled me into a hug. "You ready?"

"As I'll ever be," I said, hugging her tightly.

We walked toward my parents' bedroom. My fingers brushed along the wall as we reached the door—familiar, worn, full of memories.

Patrick gently opened it and stepped aside so Sienna could enter first. The soft morning light streamed in, casting warm stripes across the bedspread. The room smelled faintly of floral perfume—Mum's signature scent.

Sienna paused, breathing in deeply. "It still smells like her," she said quietly. "That sweet perfume she always wore… it's like she's still here."

The scent wrapped around us like a hug from the past. I nodded, my voice catching. "Yeah."

Patrick gave my hand a gentle squeeze and looked at us with tenderness. "I'll leave you both to it. I'm heading to the hardware store to grab paint samples… and maybe box up a few things at my place. You two have this."

Sienna gave him a wave. "Good luck. Don't come back with 'eggplant' walls or anything tragic."

He laughed and kissed me on the temple before slipping out.

We stood in the quiet for a moment. Then I opened the wardrobe—the same one Mum used to organise down to the last button. We started slowly, pulling items out one at a time—dresses, scarves, old cardigans. Every fold held a memory.

"This one," Sienna said, holding up a powder-blue sweater, "she wore this to your graduation."

"She cried through the whole ceremony," I smiled. "Even during the speeches."

We found a silk scarf Mum had bought on our trip to New Zealand—the only holiday we ever took together as a family. It was soft and cream-coloured, embroidered with delicate vines.

I held it to my nose. "It still smells like her."

Sienna helped me drape it gently into a keepsake box we'd set aside. "We'll make sure it's always safe."

As we worked, the room slowly transformed. The air wasn't

heavy anymore. Laughter broke through tears, like when we found an old pair of Dad's reading glasses tangled with a travel brochure for Tokyo, or a faded shopping list scribbled on the back of a postcard.

When we pulled out the photo albums from under the bed, we sat on the carpet and flipped through them slowly.

There was one of Dad doing yoga in the backyard, awkwardly twisted and grinning at the camera. Another of Mum, sunburned and laughing on a beach towel. And one of the three of us was in matching Christmas pyjamas, looking far too pleased with ourselves.

Sienna chuckled, pointing to one of Dad's failed yoga poses. "He really thought Downward Dog was a push-up."

I smiled, running my hand over the page. "These are memories I'll never forget."

She looked over at me. "Neither will I."

As I placed the last stack of photo albums into the box marked "Keep," my hand brushed something tucked behind the bed frame. A thin, timeworn envelope, sealed with a sticker shaped like a daisy. Curious, I pulled it out and slid my finger beneath the flap. Inside was a single photograph—slightly faded but still sharp enough to make my breath catch.

It was Mum and Dad.

But not the posed kind I'd grown up seeing. This one had

been snapped in a moment of pure, candid joy—Dad had Mum up on his back, both of them soaked to the skin, laughing like children caught in the rain. Her head was thrown back. He was grinning, eyes crinkled, mouth open mid-laugh.

I stared at it, stunned. "I've never seen this one," I whispered.

Sienna looked over my shoulder. "God… look at them."

"They look… young. And wild." I traced my thumb along the edge of the photo. "I don't think I ever really imagined them like this."

Sienna said nothing, just watched me quietly as I propped the photo against the windowsill. Outside, the sky had softened to a muted gold.

I moved to the bedside table and opened the bottom drawer, one I hadn't touched in years. Inside was a dusty stack of CDs— my mum's old collection. I smiled at the titles. She used to play them while cooking, humming along with a wooden spoon in hand. I pulled out one and slid it into the stereo by the dresser. The player clicked and whirred to life.

A soft piano intro filled the room, rich and familiar.

"'Come Away with Me,'" I said, eyes closed. "She loved this one."

As the music swelled, Sienna reached for my hand and gave it a gentle squeeze. We stood still, letting the melody soak into the space around us. The scent of Mum's perfume still lingered, the golden hour light spilling in, and the room somehow felt suspended in time, past and present holding hands. Then I felt it. A flutter. Strange and delicate, like a butterfly wing brushing from the inside.

I gasped, a hand flying to my belly. "What?" Sienna asked, wide-eyed.

I said nothing—just reached for her hand and guided it to the small swell beneath my shirt. We waited. Then, there it was again. A tiny, rolling nudge.

Sienna's mouth fell open. "Was that—?"

"The baby," I whispered, eyes brimming.

We both stayed like that for a long moment, music playing softly in the background, the photo of my parents watching over us, the past wrapped around the future in a single breath of time. And just like that, the room wasn't just a memory anymore.

It was alive—with love. With movement. With the promise of something new.

"I'm glad we did this together," I said softly.

"You were never going to do it alone," she replied.

Later that afternoon, with most of the room sorted into boxes and bags, we stood back and looked around. It didn't feel like goodbye—it felt like making space for new beginnings. For the tiny life we were about to welcome.

She gave me a long, lingering hug before stepping out into the hallway. "I'll let myself out. Call me if you need me, okay?"

I nodded, too full to speak.

Once she was gone, I stayed behind, sinking slowly into Mum's old armchair in the corner of the room. I curled into it like I used to as a little girl when I couldn't sleep and would find her reading here at night.

The light filtering through the curtains was golden now, touching everything with a softness that felt like peace.

I looked around the half-packed room and placed my hand gently on my belly.

"We're getting there," I whispered. "One box at a time."

Chapter 21

Packing Up The Past

Patrick stood in the middle of the small two-bedroom rental he and his dad had moved into after his mum passed away.

It wasn't fancy. The carpet was worn in places, the curtains never quite hung right, and the shower had a temperamental drip. But it had been theirs—a quiet place to rebuild when everything else had been torn down by grief.

One room had been his. The other, his dad's. After his mum died, they'd sold the family home to cover medical bills and moved here to start fresh, just the two of them. It had never really felt like home, but it had been safe. Familiar. Now, it was time to let it go.

Patrick moved methodically, boxing up only what mattered. He didn't need much, just enough to take with him to Lucy's. A few clothes. His records. Books. The framed photo of his parents that hung on the wall. His dad's old mug, chipped and comforting.

In his dad's room, the air still held a trace of him—shaving cream and laundry detergent. Patrick knelt by the wardrobe and reached under the bed. His hand found a box—dusty but carefully labelled in his dad's handwriting: Mum.

He pulled it out slowly, sitting cross-legged on the floor. For a moment, his hand hovered over the lid. He hadn't opened it since the day they packed it. Not today.

He stood, carried the box to the living room, and placed it beside the others marked to Keep. Whatever was inside, he'd open it at Lucy's, when he was ready, when he wasn't alone.

Patrick crouched beside the final box—one he hadn't opened since his dad passed. It had been sealed and pushed to the back of the wardrobe, labelled simply in faint blue ink: Keepsakes.

He opened the flaps slowly, careful not to disturb the dust that clung to the edges. Inside: an old watch wrapped in tissue, a few letters in envelopes so aged they felt like parchment… and at the bottom, nestled beneath a folded handkerchief, was a cassette tape.

"Patrick – For one day, when you're ready," was scrawled across the label in his dad's handwriting.

His breath caught. His fingers trembled as he picked it up, heart thudding with the weight of what it might hold. He sat back on his heels, staring at it like it might vanish.

There was no cassette player in sight—not anymore. But he knew Lucy's house had one. Her dad had been sentimental about things like that. He set the tape gently beside his framed photo of his parents.

Then he whispered, barely audible, "I'm not ready yet, but maybe one day, maybe when our baby arrives."

His own bedroom packed up quickly. Years of living lightly meant there wasn't much to take. He chose only what felt like pieces of him—things that would belong in the life he was building now.

He sat down on the edge of his old bed, the mattress springs groaning under his weight. The room looked even smaller now than it had when he was a teenager. Posters long gone, the pale blue paint was peeling slightly near the corners.

His eyes landed on a small crack in the ceiling he used to stare at when sleep wouldn't come, after Mum died, especially. So many nights lying there in silence, trying not to cry loud enough for Dad to hear.

He let out a slow breath and looked around. "I'm leaving, Mum," he said quietly, voice almost too soft to hear. "I think I found it—what you and Dad always wanted for me. A life. A home. Someone who makes me feel like I'm exactly where I'm supposed to be."

His throat tightened.

"I wish you could've met her. You'd love her. She's stubborn and messy and kind, and she makes me feel like I'm not broken anymore."

His voice cracked on the last word, and he dropped his head into his hands, fingers threading through his hair. A few deep breaths, a trembling exhale.

"I miss you. I miss both of you. But I'm going to be a dad now. And I promise—I'm going to give this baby everything I had from you. And more."

He sat there for a few more moments, letting the silence settle around him like a warm blanket. Then he stood, gave the room one last look, and whispered, "Thank you."

He knew he had to leave parts of his past behind to move forward—to be truly at peace. Now, the house felt empty. Not sad. Just still. He did a final walk-through, switching off lights, running his hand over the hallway wall where his growth chart used to be—scratched pencil lines marking birthdays now faded into paint. He left the keys in an envelope by the sink and closed the door behind him. As Patrick carried the last box to the car, the screen door across the street creaked open.

"Patrick?" came the voice—warm, familiar.

He turned to see Mrs. Langley, their elderly neighbour, wrapped in a chunky knitted cardigan, her hair pulled back in its usual bun. She'd brought over countless meals after his mum died, and again when his dad passed. Always checking in, always kind.

She walked to the edge of her lawn, squinting at the box in his arms. "Looks like today's the day, huh?"

He gave her a small smile. "Yeah. Time to move on."

She nodded, her expression soft. "Your dad would be proud of you. He used to tell me how strong you were—even when you didn't feel like it. And your mum? She'd be thrilled to know you found someone to love. She always wanted that for you."

Patrick's throat tightened. He swallowed hard. "Thanks,

Mrs. Langley. That… means a lot."

She stepped a little closer and lowered her voice. "I saw the picture you posted. The baby." A smile spread across her face. "You're going to be a wonderful father, Patrick."

He blinked back the sting in his eyes. "I hope so."

"You will," she said firmly. "You've already got the most important part down. You care."

She reached into her pocket and handed him a small envelope. "A little something for the baby. Just a card, but… well, I couldn't let you go without saying goodbye."

He took it, heart aching with gratitude. "Thank you."

"Take care of that girl," she added with a knowing twinkle in her eye. "And yourself."

Patrick nodded. "I will. Promise."

When he pulled into Lucy's driveway, the sky was streaked with gold. He carried the boxes inside quietly. The house already felt warmer—lived in, loved.

He didn't call out. He didn't need to. He found Lucy in the nursery, curled up in the armchair that had once belonged to her mum, wrapped in the soft scarf he'd draped over her the day before. Her eyes were closed, one hand resting on her belly. She looked like peace itself—soft, quiet, and glowing in the dusky light.

Patrick stood in the doorway for a moment, watching her. Then he crossed the room, crouched beside her, and pressed a kiss to her temple.

"I'm home," he whispered. Tomorrow, they'd unpack.

Tomorrow, they'd go through the box labelled Mum.

But tonight, Patrick just sat beside her, resting his hand over hers, grounding himself in this new chapter. The past was behind him. And now, finally, he knew where he belonged.

Chapter 22

Her Words, His Heart

I couldn't believe I'd fallen asleep in Mum's old armchair. The soft scarf was still wrapped around my shoulders, her scent faint but present. When I glanced down, I found Patrick asleep on the floor next to me, his back against the chair.

I nudged him gently.

He stirred, then looked up at me with a sleepy smile. "Morning, gorgeous."

"Morning, sexy. How did you go packing up your place yesterday? Sorry, I crashed before you got back."

He stretched, his back cracking faintly. "Yeah, it was okay. Sad, but it needed to be done. I brought a few boxes, and one I need to go through. I don't really know what's inside. I remember Dad and I packing it up after Mum died, but he kept adding to it. I found it sealed under his bed."

"Let's go downstairs, make some coffee, and open it together," I said.

I made the coffee while Patrick carried the box to the dining room table. We sat side by side as steam rose from our mugs.

He opened the box slowly. Right on top was a photo. He held it up, eyes already glistening.

"This is my parents on their wedding day."

"They look so happy," I said softly.

"Yeah. They were."

Beneath the photo lay his mum's wedding veil—a delicate, white lace with tiny pearl beading. Absolutely beautiful.

Next came a folded blanket. Patrick ran his hand over it.

"This is the blanket my mum used on the couch. I remember crawling into her lap and snuggling under it while she read to me." He looked over at me. "Maybe we can use it on your mum's chair in the nursery."

I nodded, tears rolling down my cheeks. "Perfect."

Then, at the very bottom, was a small velvet box. Patrick opened it slowly, not knowing what to expect.

Tears spilled down his face. "It's her rings. All three pieces of her bridal set."

He turned them toward me—vintage, intricate, stunning.

He looked at me curiously. "What happened to your parents' rings?"

I smiled faintly. "I buried them wearing their rings. So they could stay married in the afterlife."

He smiled and gently closed the ring box.

"There was something else," Patrick said, lifting a small, dusty cassette from the bottom of the box. It was labelled in soft, cursive handwriting: For you, both.

"Do you even have a cassette player?" I asked, brushing my fingers over the label.

"My dad's is in the attic," he murmured, holding it like something sacred. "We'll listen… when we're ready."

As he looked back into the main box, thinking it was empty, his eyes caught something else.

A white envelope.

He took a deep breath and opened it.

To my brave boy, Patrick,

If you're reading this, then cancer has taken me and I'm no longer by your side. I asked your father to give you this when you found love—endless love, like I found with your father.

Now that your eyes are reading my words, I hope it's true. I hope you've found a love as strong as ours. I hope you've found the one who makes you smile, even on your darkest days.

If you have, hold her tight and never let go.

Take every adventure that comes your way. Treat every day like it's your last—no one ever knows when their last breath will come.

But for you, my brave boy, I wish a long, happy, and rewarding life. One filled with love, laughter, and babies. I always wanted to be a grandmother.

Follow your dreams.

Until we meet again, I love you, Mum.

P.S. I asked Dad to give you my rings, in the hope that when you found the right girl, you'd give them to her.

Patrick broke.

I held him as he cried, the letter clutched in his hand. Deeper than I'd ever seen. Raw and unfiltered. Eventually, he stood, returning the veil and letter to the box. The small velvet ring box, however, he slipped into his pocket. He thought it slipped by me. It didn't.

He picked up the blanket and the wedding photo and walked them quietly to the nursery. He placed the blanket on the armchair and set the photo next to the one of my parents.

"Now they can all look over our baby," he said softly. Just then, the doorbell rang.

"Were you expecting someone?" he asked.

"No. You?"

I walked to the door and opened it to find Sienna, holding a brown paper bag and a gift.

"I brought you lunch," she said, grinning. "And a onesie."

I laughed. "I don't think the onesie will fit me."

"No, silly." She laughed. "It's for the baby!"

Patrick greeted her with a smile, then disappeared upstairs to keep working on the nursery.

As we unpacked the food, I filled Sienna in on what we'd found in the box, especially the rings.

"He put them in his pocket," I said, voice quiet. "Didn't think I noticed."

Sienna grinned, her eyes already misty. "Oh, honey. I think he knows exactly what he's doing."

After lunch and laughter, and a few quiet moments just sitting in the nursery, Sienna finally stood.

"I should go," she said, hugging me tightly. "But promise me you'll text me if you need anything—even if it's just someone to tell you you're glowing."

I laughed and nodded, walking her to the door. The house was quiet again. I wandered upstairs and found Patrick in the nursery, placing a tiny teddy bear on the shelf. He turned when he heard me, that familiar warmth lighting up his face.

"Everything okay?" he asked.

I nodded. "Better than okay."

I crossed the room slowly, not saying a word, just watching him—this man I loved more than I ever thought possible. He looked a little tired. A little worn. But still, so completely mine.

And I wanted him.

"Come with me," I said, my voice lower than usual. He blinked in surprise, but followed.

We moved to the bedroom, and I didn't wait. I turned to him, tugged gently at the hem of his shirt. "Let me take care of you tonight."

His hands reached for me, but I stopped him. "No," I whispered. "Just let me."

His breath hitched as I undressed him slowly—his shirt first, then the rest—reverently, deliberately. I kissed along his jaw, his collarbone, his chest, trailing my hands over the familiar lines of his body. The man who had held me through loss, who had loved me without fear. Tonight, I wanted to show him just how much he meant to me.

When he tried to touch me again, I caught his hands, laced my fingers through his, and pressed them to the pillow above his head as I climbed on top of him.

His mouth parted, eyes dark with heat. "Lucy…"

I leaned in, my lips brushing his. "Let me love you, Patrick. My way."

And then I did.

I traced a line down his chest with my fingertips, feeling him shiver beneath my touch. Every inch of him belonged to me tonight—my hands, my pace, my rhythm. He watched me, breath shallow, surrendering without resistance. And I… I was undone by how much he trusted me.

I took my time—every kiss, every touch, a promise. I moved with slow, intentional rhythm, guiding him, claiming him. He let go completely beneath me, eyes locked with mine the entire time.

It was powerful. Not just the sex, but the connection. The way I could feel his surrender. The way I knew—without a doubt—that I was safe, desired, in control.

When we both reached that final, shuddering release, it wasn't with words. Just shared breath. A tangle of limbs. A hush that said everything.

Afterwards, I curled into his chest, heart still racing.

Patrick pressed his lips to my forehead. "I don't think I'll ever recover from that."

I smiled into his skin. "Good. I know it's a moment I'll never forget."

"I honestly never thought I'd have this," he murmured.

"What?"

"A future that doesn't scare me. A love that doesn't leave."

I brushed my thumb across his cheek. "You've got both now."

We drifted to sleep, tangled together, the soft weight of love and legacy all around us. And for the first time in a long time, I didn't just feel strong.

I felt whole.

Chapter 23

Everything In One Moment

The soft hum of the sander echoed from upstairs, followed by the faint scent of fresh paint. I stood in the hallway, one hand resting on the gentle swell of my belly, the other brushing along the edge of the nursery door.

Inside, it looked almost complete.

The crib was up. The walls were a soft sage green. My mum's chair sat in the corner, draped in Patrick's mother's blanket. On the shelf were children's books, hand-folded onesies, and a photo of both our parents, watching over us, over this baby, in their own quiet way.

I stepped inside and ran my fingertips along the crib's smooth railing, pausing at the corner where Patrick had carefully sanded the edge down just the day before. I looked at the stack of picture books he'd alphabetised, the folded onesie with tiny koalas, the soft toy bunny that already looked well-loved.

I sat down in Mum's chair and let the silence settle around me. The room smelled faintly of lavender and fresh paint, and it was the first time I allowed myself to picture it fully. Not just a space, but a life. A baby nestled in my arms. Patrick was pacing the room in the middle of the night, trying to soothe cries with sleepy kisses and whispered lullabies. Story time, giggles echoing through the walls, chubby fingers tugging at hair and hearts alike.

This room wasn't just painted—it had been built with love. Layered with memory. And every inch of it carried the ghosts of the past and the pulse of a future we were stitching together from scratch.

Patrick stepped out of the room, a smudge of white paint on his cheek, his shirt clinging to his chest from the effort of the morning. His eyes met mine, and for a moment, we just looked. No words. Just that feeling we always seemed to find when the world was still and we were together.

"The nursery is nearly done," he said, wiping his hands on a rag. "Though I'm not sure it'll ever feel finished until our baby is in there."

I smiled. "You've done so much. Thank you."

He came closer, fingertips brushing my cheek. "I'd do it a thousand times over."

We stood there like that—me, barefoot in one of his old T-shirts, him sweaty and paint-covered—and somehow it felt perfect.

"I want to show you something," he said, taking my hand. "Come with me."

He led me downstairs, past the kitchen and out the back door. There, in the garden, was a small table, a white cloth fluttering in the breeze, two glasses sparkling in the sun, and my favourite flowers spilling from an old jug. It wasn't extravagant, but it felt like something out of a dream. My breath caught.

For a second, I thought maybe he was surprising me with brunch or some quiet backyard date. My heart fluttered with the sweetness of it, the effort. But then he reached into his pocket, and my heartbeat sprinted.

No. He wouldn't—

Then, he dropped to one knee.

I froze.

He pulled the ring box from his pocket—the one I'd seen him tuck away after going through his mum's things. Inside was her engagement ring—delicate, vintage, filled with meaning.

"I don't have a speech. I thought I'd want one, but now that I'm here, all I can think about is this: You've already changed my life, Lucy. Every part of it. You've brought light where there was darkness, laughter where there was silence. You've shown me what real love looks like."

He glanced at my belly, then back up at me. His eyes glistened.

"You're carrying our child. You've given me a home. A reason. A future. And I want to spend every day of it loving you. Will you marry me?"

My heart slammed into my ribs. Emotion surged in my throat. I nodded, unable to speak, tears spilling over as I whispered,

"Yes. Of course, yes."

He slid the ring onto my finger and kissed it like it meant everything.

We didn't make it back to the house.

I wrapped my arms around his neck and kissed him like he was oxygen and I was drowning. He caught on fast, backing us onto the old outdoor lounge, our bodies already knowing the rhythm. I straddled him, tugging at his shirt, our kisses deep and messy, our hands greedy.

The garden, the breeze, and the world faded.

I took the lead again—not for the first time, but with full intention this time because I needed to. Because I knew exactly how I wanted to love him. The rough fabric of the outdoor lounge scratched against my knees, the breeze tugging gently at my hair as I straddled him. I could taste the sun on his skin, salt and warmth and home. Though my body had changed, his touch reminded me of everything I still was—and everything we were together. His eyes, so dark and full of emotion, searched mine. I whispered in his ear, "I'm yours. Always."

I moved with purpose—every kiss, every roll of my hips tuned to our rhythm, to what we needed. My body felt heavier now, but never more powerful. Never more sure. When I lowered myself onto him, we both gasped. His hands gripped my hips, his head falling back. I watched every reaction as if committing it to memory.

This was homecoming. This was everything he never knew he was waiting for.

The sun dipped behind the trees as we moved together, again and again, until I forgot where my body ended and his began. After, with our bodies tangled and breath still uneven, he wrapped his arms around me and whispered into my hair:

"You make everything feel possible." It wasn't just love.

It was everything.

It was a moment I'd never forget.

Chapter 24

Just The Ones Who Matter

Wedding planning wasn't exactly what I'd imagined.

No spreadsheets. No Pinterest boards. No colour-coded guest lists.

The two of us on the back deck, bare feet up, iced tea in hand, watching the wind move through the trees and talking about the rest of our lives like it was the most natural thing in the world.

"So," Patrick said, nudging my knee with his. "Big church wedding? Ballroom? Helicopter entrance?"

I laughed. "You'd look terrible in a tux on a helipad."

He grinned. "So, something small then?"

I nodded. "Simple. Just us, Sienna, and whoever counts as 'immediate family' these days."

He fell quiet for a moment, staring out at the yard. "I've got an uncle in Brisbane. He sends me a birthday message every year and forgets my name half the time."

"I've got a cousin who asked if we were rich now that my parents are gone," I said. "We can skip them."

"Agreed."

It was a strange reality—neither of us had much family left, at least not the kind that felt like family. In the end, we didn't need a guest list. Just the people who knew our story. The ones who had stood beside us through the worst and the best.

So, that meant Sienna. And maybe Jill, if she was ready.

"I mentioned hiring the house staff back a while ago," I said, almost like I was reminding myself. "But I never followed through."

Patrick's eyes lit up with something between relief and affection. "Honestly, I've been waiting for that to happen. I didn't want to push—you've handled everything—but I think it's time. You shouldn't have to juggle everything, especially once the baby's here."

"I was thinking Jill could come back three days a week," I said. "And maybe Joe, the yard guy. You've been amazing with the lawns, but they're huge. You need to rest, too."

He exhaled, like a weight had just slipped from his shoulders. "You have no idea how happy that makes me."

I smirked. "So you're not too proud to admit you've been mentally losing arguments with the whipper snipper?"

"Daily."

We laughed, and then the conversation drifted back to the wedding.

"I don't need a big white dress," I said. "Just something simple. Something I can wear barefoot."

"I don't care what you wear," Patrick said. "As long as you walk toward me."

I turned my hand over in his, threading our fingers together. "We're going to have the most unconventional, slightly chaotic, perfectly us wedding ever."

He smiled. "And I wouldn't have it any other way." Just then, my phone rang. Sienna.

I answered on speaker.

"Well?" she said, skipping pleasantries. "What's the plan? Do I need to clear my schedule? Find a dress? Rent a llama?"

I laughed. "No llamas."

"I make no promises," she shot back. "You know, I once planned a wedding with a live owl ring bearer? I'm only saying, I've got connections."

Patrick leaned closer to the phone. "It'll be small. Backyard. Just us and the people who matter."

"Oh thank God," Sienna sighed. "I can't fake smile through another dry chicken dinner at a reception hall. But I'm giving a toast, okay? I've already written three drafts. Spoiler alert: one includes a sex pun."

"Of course it does," I muttered.

She paused for a beat. "Tell me the truth—has Patrick already Googled how to write wedding vows?"

Patrick raised an eyebrow. "Excuse you, I'm a man of words." I mouthed "barely", and Sienna cracked up.

"Oh, this is going to be good," she said. "Alright, keep me in the loop. And Lucy—don't forget to pick something hot to wear under the soft barefoot dress."

"Noted."

As the call ended and the sun slid lower in the sky, we headed into the kitchen.

"Something sexy under your dress, huh?"

I smirked. "That's what she said."

Without another word, he stood and crossed the kitchen in two strides, his hands landing on my hips as he guided me back against the counter.

"How about you show me what's under your dress… right now?"

"Patrick—" I started, but my breath caught as he lifted me effortlessly, setting me on the edge of the kitchen bench. The cool marble of the bench contrasted with the heat between us.

His body pressed between my legs, and his mouth crashed onto mine.

The kiss deepened, urgent and all-consuming. His hands slid up under my dress, fingers trailing along my thighs, coaxing a moan from my lips. The fabric bunched around my waist, forgotten.

"You drive me insane," he muttered against my skin. "Do you know what you do to me?"

I didn't answer.

I couldn't.

His touch was demanding, and my entire body was already

aching for him.

He pulled my underwear down slowly, dragging the lace along my skin like a promise.

I gasped as his fingers slid over me, knowing exactly how to unmake me.

And then—he was inside me. The world tilted.

I gripped the edge of the bench as he thrust into me—strong and sure—each movement grounding and devastating all at once. He held me firmly, his hands gripping my hips, his eyes locked on mine.

I should've said something cheeky, teased him—but all I could do was hold on as he undid me from the inside out.

"You're mine," he growled softly, voice ragged.

"Yes," I whispered. "Always."

The kitchen disappeared around us. The wedding, the baby, the lists and plans—none of it mattered. Just the way he moved inside me. The way he filled every part of me. The way we burned for each other.

My legs tightened around him, heels digging into his back as I chased the edge. He was right there with me, meeting me thrust for thrust, breath for breath—until we both shattered in unison, clinging to each other like the world was ending.

We stayed like that for a long time—our bodies trembling, his head resting on my shoulder, my fingers tangled in his hair.

Eventually, he lifted his head and kissed me softly.

"You know," he murmured, brushing a hand along my thigh, "Sienna might be onto something."
I laughed. "I'll be sure to wear something really sexy under my wedding dress."

He smirked. "Or nothing at all."

Our breathing slowed, sweat cooling against our skin. He brushed a strand of hair from my forehead and kissed the corner of my mouth.

"You alright?" he whispered.

"More than," I said, fingers still trailing along his spine.

He gently tugged my dress back down, smoothing the fabric over my thighs with a kind of reverence that made me ache all over again.

"Think the baby's traumatised?" I teased. Patrick grinned, eyes soft.

"Or impressed."

I chuckled. "First memory might be the sound of me moaning on the kitchen counter."

He pressed his lips to my belly. "We'll explain it when they're thirty."

Chapter 25

Satin And Sass

The days after the proposal passed in a blur of bridal planning and belly growth.

The nursery was nearly done, invites were sent, and Sienna and I had one main goal for the day: find the perfect wedding dress—and something sexy for the wedding night.

Somewhere along the way, we also detoured into maternity bras—because my boobs were staging a full-blown rebellion.

We found the dress first.

Ivory silk, fitted across the bust with a dreamy, flowing skirt that draped over my belly like it had been designed just for me.

I stood in the change room, one hand on my bump, and nearly cried.

"I feel like a pregnant goddess," I whispered.

Sienna wiped a tear. "You are a pregnant goddess. Buy the damn dress."

As I stood there, one hand on my belly, a thought hit me— this was supposed to be Mum's moment too. She would've cried. She would've fussed over every detail and insisted I needed "something blue."

"She'd love this dress," I said quietly.
Sienna didn't ask who I meant. She just nodded, eyes

shining.

Next stop: lingerie.

That's where things got funny.

We walked out of the boutique with two very different bags.

One held delicate, lacy white lingerie—sexy, sheer, with a matching silk robe I didn't know I needed.

The other? Three industrial-strength maternity bras with more support than my emotional state.

Sienna looked between the two bags and burst out laughing. "You're literally holding your dual personality in each hand.

Bag one says, 'bend me over and praise my curves.' Bag two says, 'I need stability and zero underwire pain.'"

I   doubled over. "Why am I buying maternity bras and crotchless panties in the same hour?"

"Because pregnancy is chaos, and you're doing amazing." We were still laughing as we exited the shop, and practically collided with a familiar voice. "Well. That's quite a combination."

Zeke.

He stood just a few steps away, eyes flicking between my shopping bags and my bump, eyebrows raised like he had a right to comment.

I straightened.

Sienna stepped up like a lioness on guard.

"No one gets to talk to my best friend the way you did," she snapped. "Not then, not now, not ever."

I put a hand on her arm. "It's okay." Then I met Zeke's eyes, unshaken.

"Technically," I said, "he didn't get away with it. He got punched in the jaw by Patrick."

Zeke winced.

"I deserved it."

"You did," I said calmly.

He looked me over again. "So, you're really marrying him? And having his baby?"

I raised the lingerie bag.

"Does it look like I'm not?"

He flinched but tried to cover it.

"You were everything to me. You still belong with me."

I smiled. "I belong with whoever I choose. And I didn't choose you."

I patted my belly.

"And yes, I'm having his baby. This isn't a balloon. It kicks. A lot."

Zeke opened his mouth, but nothing came out. For once, he had no clever retort.

Sienna smirked and linked arms with me. "Time to go."

We walked off like a movie ending. In the car, I texted

Patrick.

"Shopping complete. Sexy lingerie acquired. Maternity bras, too. Guess which one's not for you?"

His reply was almost instant.

"I'll pretend to be surprised. Did Sienna make you try on anything scandalous?"

Sienna snapped a photo of the lingerie bag dangling beside my belly.

"Caption this: Hot Mama vibes with bonus milk jugs incoming."

I snorted. "You're unhinged."

"You love it," she said. "Admit it. You're living your best ROM-com life."

And just like that, the day melted into laughter and love, and just enough sass to keep things interesting.

Back home, I found Patrick in the laundry, sorting a basket of clothes. He looked up as I walked in, a smirk tugging at his lips when he saw the two bags dangling from my fingers.

"You're back," he said, walking over to kiss me. "Shopping success?"

I held up the bags. "One's full of sexy lingerie. The other is... maternity bras. Basically, two sides of the same hormonal coin."

He chuckled, shaking his head. "You're impossible—and

perfect."

He turned back to folding clothes, completely unaware of the slow-burning thoughts forming in my mind. His shirt was riding up as he reached to grab a basket, exposing just enough of his lower back to make me ache for more. I stepped up behind him and ran my hand slowly under his shirt.

"You know," I whispered, lips near his ear, "Sienna said I should do something sexy before the wedding."

"Oh?" he asked, voice roughening, pausing with a sock in one hand.

"Yeah." I pushed him gently against the dryer and kissed his jaw.

"Want to help me follow through?"

He turned to face me, and in one swift move, he lifted me onto the running washing machine. The hum of the spin cycle vibrated under me, sending delicious ripples through my thighs. His hands found my waist, and I wrapped my legs around him, pulling him in close.

"You're wearing one of the new things, aren't you?" he murmured, tugging at the hem of my dress, voice low and hungry.

"Maybe," I teased, sliding the fabric up my thighs. "Wanna see?"

He didn't need another word.

His hands slid up my legs, parting them as he pressed himself between them, kissing me with heat that made me dizzy.

The rhythm of the washing machine matched the growing pulse between my legs, and when he finally pushed aside my panties and entered me, it was slow, deep, and utterly consuming.

The laundry walls echoed with our gasps and moans as he moved inside me, his mouth exploring my neck, my chest, my lips.

Every movement, every sound, every breath was pure fire—raw and real, the kind of sex that made time bend.

"God, Lucy…" he groaned, gripping my hips as I tightened around him, riding each wave as if we were made for this moment.

"I love you," I gasped, head falling back, heels digging into his back.

His lips brushed my ear. "Forever."

And when it was over—when the shaking subsided and our breathing slowed—he rested his forehead against mine, still holding me close, his fingers tracing lazy circles on my thighs.

"Best laundry day ever," he whispered.

I laughed breathlessly, still catching my breath.

"You really think we're ready for all this?" I whispered.

Patrick brushed hair from my face. "Not even a little. But I'd rather be unready with you than ready with anyone else."

I smiled, heart full. "That's the right answer."

"You're always the right answer."

"Sienna's gonna want details."

"I'll let you exaggerate," he said, brushing a kiss to my lips. "You're better at the dramatic storytelling."

I tucked my head into his shoulder, the rumble of the washer still soft beneath me.

It wasn't just sex. It was a moment—another one I'd never forget.

Chapter 26

Given With Love

The morning of the wedding arrived with golden light streaming through the bedroom windows, and my very prominent belly reminding me that everything about today needed to be a little more carefully planned.

My dress—thankfully altered by a miracle-working seamstress—hung on the back of the door, waiting, like I was, to become something more than just a dream.

Sienna arrived just after breakfast, carrying a coffee, a bag of emergency bobby pins, and the same fierce determination she had the day of my parents' funeral.

"All right," she said, kicking the door shut behind her, "I'm here to make sure you don't fall apart. Or throw up on your wedding dress."

"I feel like I already did both," I groaned, fidgeting with my robe.

She grinned. "Hormones or nerves?"

"Both. And grief," I whispered. "They won't be there. My dad won't walk me down the aisle. My mum won't be in the front row smiling through her tears."

Sienna crossed the room and cupped my cheeks. "Then I'll

walk you. I'll give you away."

I blinked at her, lips trembling. "You'd do that?"

"Of course," she said. "Even though we both know I'm not really giving you to him. I'm just willing to share you."

We both laughed, and I let the tears come—because I knew she'd hold me through every one of them. Hair curled, dress zipped, and belly beautifully framed beneath lace and silk, I turned to her.

"Do I look okay in this?"

Sienna stepped back, eyes wide with emotion.

"You look like everything your parents would be proud of. And hot. Let's not forget hot."

Sienna opened a small velvet box, revealing a delicate silver bracelet with a single sapphire nestled in the centre.

"Something blue," she said. "I know you're not superstitious, but… your mum would've made sure you had it. So I figured someone had to."

The tears came fast.

I looked down at the bracelet, then up at her. "I actually had a thought of needing something blue when we were dress shopping, how did you know?"

She shrugged. "Because I know you. And because you would've done the same for me."

She clipped the bracelet onto my wrist and kissed my cheek, both of us blinking back tears.

"You've got this," she whispered.

And for the first time that day, I truly felt like I did. Downstairs, Patrick was already waiting in the garden.

The backyard had been transformed into something out of a storybook—simple white chairs, scattered petals along the makeshift aisle, soft music floating through the late afternoon air.

It was perfect.

Small. Intimate. Full of love.

The guest list was short. Just a few family members and friends—including our lovely housekeeper, Jill, and Joe the groundskeeper, who had both become like family again.

Sienna's parents sat in the second row, beaming with pride. Beside them was Sienna's date—a kind-eyed paramedic named Travis, whom she'd brought mainly so she wouldn't have to slow dance alone.

As the music shifted, Sienna looped her arm through mine and whispered,

"Ready?"

"Not at all."

"Perfect. Let's go."

The moment I stepped out, I saw him.

Patrick.

Standing beneath the arbor, dressed in a perfectly tailored

suit, his hands trembling at his sides, eyes already glassy.

The second he saw me, he broke.

Tears slipped down his cheeks, but he smiled through every one of them, like he'd never seen anything more beautiful.

I smiled back and nodded to the guests, my heart full.

When we reached him, Sienna didn't let go immediately. She turned to Patrick and said—loud enough for everyone to hear—"If you hurt her, if you break her—I'll kill you."

Everyone laughed, and Patrick gave her a solemn nod. "Understood."

Then she kissed my cheek and placed my hand into his. "Take good care of each other," she said.

And just like that, I was home again.

She stepped aside, dabbing her eyes with a tissue, and the celebrant began.

I barely heard the first few words—too focused on the man standing in front of me.

His eyes never left mine. He looked hot. He always did. But today, under the golden afternoon light, with our baby growing between us, Patrick looked like everything I'd ever prayed for.

When it was time for the vows, Patrick took both my hands and cleared his throat, blinking away tears.

"I didn't believe in fate before you," he said softly. "But I believe in it now. Because only fate would have brought us together in the middle of so much grief and made it feel like hope. You have this way of making the world quieter, softer— like I can finally breathe."

He glanced down at my belly, then back into my eyes.

"You're my home, Lucy. You're my reason. And I vow to love you with every part of me, for every moment we get. Through late-night feeds and early-morning chaos. Through joy, loss, and growth. Through everything."

Tears slipped freely down my cheeks.

I inhaled deeply, then smiled through the emotion.

"You found me when I didn't know I was lost," I began. "You loved me when I wasn't sure I'd ever be able to find love. You saw something in me that made me want to keep going. And now, you are my path. My peace. My reason to keep going."

I squeezed his hands gently.

"I vow to love you not just in the easy moments, but in the hard ones. In the tired, the messy, and the overwhelming. I vow to stand beside you, even when our world changes. I vow to build a life that feels like us. Full of laughter, warmth, and tiny feet on the floors of our home."

Patrick was crying openly now. So was Sienna. So was Jill.

The celebrant smiled through her own tears and pronounced us husband and wife. When Patrick leaned in to kiss me, it felt like time slowed. Like every breath, every heartbeat, every ache that had ever lived in my chest dissolved into this one perfect moment. We didn't have a first dance. Not because we didn't want one, but because Sienna insisted on grabbing my hand the second the music started and twirling me around the garden like we were fifteen again, dancing in her bedroom with hairbrushes as microphones.

Patrick joined in, of course—stealing me away with a dramatic spin that ended in a kiss—and somehow, our small backyard reception turned into a joyful, barefoot garden party.

There were fairy lights and finger food, champagne flutes filled with lemonade, and soft music echoing through the trees. Sienna's date, Travis, was charming and full of good rhythm, much to her delight.

Jill floated in and out with trays of food, her cheeks rosy with happiness. Joe—ever the gentleman—stood near the barbecue, flipping sausages and telling terrible dad jokes to anyone who'd listen.

Everyone was relaxed, smiling, and present.

Later, under a canopy of string lights in the backyard, Sienna tapped her glass with a fork and stood, a slightly wicked grin on her face.

"I'm going to keep this short, because if I start sobbing like a drunk bridesmaid, I won't stop."

Laughter rippled through the guests.

"I've known Lucy for almost our entire lives. She's the kind of person who gives you the last slice of cake, even though you know she secretly wanted it. She's fierce, smart, and loyal to a fault… which is why, when Patrick came along, I gave him a hard time."

She paused, looking at Patrick pointedly.

"You passed the tests, mate. Even the ones you didn't know you were taking."

More laughter.

"But in all seriousness, watching the two of you has been… healing. Beautiful. Messy and chaotic and exactly what love is supposed to look like. Lucy, your mum and dad would be so damn proud of you. Of the life you're building. And Patrick— thank you for loving her the way she deserves."

She raised her glass. "To the kind of love that rebuilds. That softens. That laughs in the middle of a disaster and dances barefoot in the kitchen. To Lucy and Patrick."

Glasses clinked. My heart threatened to burst.

Sienna sat beside me and grabbed my hand under the table. "I meant every word," she whispered.

I squeezed back. "So did I. When I chose you to stand beside me today and every other day of our lives."

The dancing continued and as I stood back near the arbor, watching it all unfold. The lights were glowing now, soft and warm, casting halos over our guests. My belly was heavy, but my heart even heavier—with joy, with love, with everything that had brought us here.

Patrick came up behind me, wrapping his arms around my waist and resting his chin on my shoulder.

"You okay, Mrs. Lawson?"

I turned my head and kissed his jaw. "More than okay."

"I don't know if we'll have a wedding album filled with extravagant photos," he said quietly. "But this… this feels perfect."

"It is perfect," I whispered.

And as the sun began to dip below the horizon and fairy lights twinkled overhead, I knew—this day, this night, these people—would become another moment I'd never forget.

Chapter 27

Our Wildest Night, Our Next Beginning

The house was dimly lit with the soft glow of candles flickering on shelves and benchtops, casting golden shadows against the walls. We didn't rush. We didn't speak. There was only the electricity between us—the awareness that this was our wedding night. And we were finally husband and wife.

Patrick kissed me like I was everything he'd ever waited for, and I kissed him like I never wanted to stop.

It started in the hallway—my back against the wall, his hands memorising every curve of my body. We barely made it to the living room before his jacket was on the floor, my dress pushed up to my hips, and his lips were trailing heat across my collarbone.

Then came the kitchen—he lifted me onto the counter, kissed me breathless, and whispered things only I was meant to hear.

We stumbled, laughing and gasping, into the lounge room next. Couch cushions were pushed aside, clothes scattered, skin pressed to skin.

By the time we made it to the bedroom, we were both undone. And yet, somehow, just getting started.

It wasn't just sex. It was something far more intimate—skin to skin, soul to soul. Raw, consuming, slow and wild all at once. We made love like we were etching memories into each other's skin. Every movement felt like a promise, like this night would live with us forever.

And it would be a moment I'll never forget.

I woke up tangled in white sheets, the golden light of morning pouring through the windows. Patrick lay beside me, one hand resting protectively on my belly, the other still holding mine.

"Hey, Mrs. Lawson," he murmured, his voice thick with sleep.

I smiled, brushing a strand of hair from his forehead. "That still feels surreal."

He kissed my knuckles. "It's real. You're mine. I'm yours."

For a long moment, we didn't move—just soaked in the stillness of a new beginning. His thumb traced circles against the ring he'd given me.

"I wonder what our baby will be like," I whispered, glancing at my belly. "Our little one."

"I hope Bub gets your heart," he said softly. "And your stubbornness. Though that might kill me."

I laughed, curling into him. "You love it."

"God help me, I really do."

The next few weeks blurred in a swirl of baby preparations. Last-minute tasks we'd pushed off now took over our days—washing tiny onesies, hanging wall art in the nursery, reorganising cupboards, stocking nappies, assembling the pram.

Jill came three times a week to help, and Joe kept the lawns trimmed like clockwork.

Sienna was over almost every other day. She helped hang curtains, fold baby clothes, and tease me mercilessly about nesting.

"You cleaned out your spice drawer. Lucy."

"The spices, yes. Of course I did."

"It needed doing!" I defended myself.

"So does my love life," Sienna muttered.

I grinned. "Well, I can't help you there, but I can tell you about my wedding night."

She froze mid-fold. "Okay. Yes. Go on."

I leaned in, whispering just enough to make her eyes widen and cheeks flush. "There were candles, multiple rooms. A countertop that may never recover. A lot of kissing. Possibly some furniture that will never feel the same again."

Sienna let out a dramatic gasp. "You did the newlywed world tour in your own house!"

I giggled. "It was… more intimate than I expected. But also more intense. There was this moment when we were in the hallway, and he just looked at me like I was his entire world."

Her teasing softened into something warm. "You deserve that kind of love. And all the hallway sex too."

"Actually, I have an idea I might be able to help you with

your love life, let's go on a double date!"

Sienna agreed it was worth a try.

Sienna brought Travis—they have been going steady since my wedding, but Sienna still wasn't convinced he was the one. We went to a candlelit bistro, tucked into a quiet corner booth. Over mains, we laughed more than we ate. Sienna and I shared a chocolate lava cake while Patrick and Travis compared travel horror stories.

Then I looked at her, raised a brow, and said, "So… how's your Eiffel Tower?"

Sienna nearly choked on her drink. "Lucy!"

Patrick looked confused until I smirked and added, "You remember how Sienna said you were my Eiffel Tower? Just wondering if Travis… measures up."

Travis's ears turned red. Sienna, mortified, burst out laughing.

"Only you would ask that in front of the men themselves," she said, shaking her head.

Patrick grinned. "She's bold. That's one of the many reasons I married her."

We toasted to that. Then I froze.

"Oh. Oh no."

"What?" Patrick asked, instantly alert.

"Either I just wet myself here at the table… or my water just broke."

Sienna dropped her spoon. "Right now? Like right now?"

I looked down at the puddle beneath me and nodded. "Yep. Show's starting early, folks."

Patrick was already on his feet, napkins flying, panic and excitement in his eyes. "Okay. Okay. Hospital. Let's go. Now."

Travis waved down the waiter with wide eyes. Sienna was already helping me to my feet, grabbing my handbag, and steadying me with one arm.

"I've got you," she said. "Let's meet your baby."

Patrick appeared at my other side in an instant, his hand sliding around my back like it was the most natural thing in the world.

"Car's out front," he said breathlessly. "I texted the hospital. We're ready."

We made our way out of the restaurant, leaving behind soaked seats, half-eaten desserts, and a very confused waiter holding a receipt no one would ever look at.

Outside, the air was cooler, calmer somehow—as if the whole world knew everything was about to change.

The moment we hit the car, it turned into a comedy of nerves.

Patrick fumbled with the keys twice before finally unlocking the doors. I slid into the back seat while Sienna climbed in beside me, practically holding my hand hostage as the first real contraction hit.

"Ow. Okay. That was not a practice one," I hissed through gritted teeth.

Sienna immediately started timing it on her phone. "One minute, twenty-four seconds. That's the real deal."

Patrick glanced at us through the rear-view mirror. "Do we need music? Soothing playlist? No, too weird. Maybe silence is better?"

"Patrick," I said, exhaling, "just focus on not missing the hospital."

"Right. Right. Ten and two on the wheel."

Sienna looked over at me and whispered, "Remember that time we got stuck in traffic and almost peed ourselves? This is so much worse."

I let out a half-laugh, half-groan as another contraction rolled through. "You're not wrong."

Because this was it.

It was happening.

From hallway sex to hospital chaos, these were the moments I'd never forget."

With soaked seats, nervous laughter, and hearts that had never been more ready.

Chapter 28

The Moment She Arrived

The hospital room was filled with the beeping of machines, fluorescent lights buzzing overhead, and the low hum of anxious breath. Patrick held one of my hands, Sienna clutched the other. My back arched, sweat dripped down my temples, and my entire body was on fire. Literal fire.

"Her head's right there, Lucy. You've got this," the midwife said calmly.

But nothing about this felt calm. "My vagina is on fire!" I screamed.

Patrick squeezed my hand tighter, his face pale but full of unwavering support. "You're doing amazing. Just breathe, baby. You're almost there."

"Breathe?" I glared at him, then turned to Sienna. "I swear, if he says breathe one more time, I'm going to throw a bedpan at him."

Sienna laughed and wiped my forehead. "I've got your back. You yell, I'll aim."

Another contraction ripped through me, and I screamed, bearing down with everything I had left.

Time slowed—just for a second.

I shut my eyes, and in the dark behind my lids, I saw her. Mum.

In our old kitchen, hair wrapped in a scarf, tea in hand, smiling like she always did when she knew I was stronger than I believed.

"You've got this, Luce," she seemed to say. "You always did."

"One more big push!" the midwife called.

I closed my eyes, held onto the voices that grounded me, and pushed.

My legs were shaking. My throat raw. I could feel every inch of her, every heartbeat, and it felt like my body was tearing and rebuilding all at once.

And then… silence.

A cry.

A perfect, beautiful cry that shattered the tension in the room and rebuilt it into something brand new.

"Congratulations, it's a girl," the midwife said, still calm, like she hadn't just witnessed an exorcism.

"She's here," Patrick whispered, his voice breaking. Our daughter.

The midwife gently placed her on my chest. She was red and wrinkly and perfect.

Tiny fists, button nose, a soft patch of dark hair—she was

every dream I'd never dared speak aloud.

I looked down and saw her tiny fist curl around the chain of the locket I'd worn—Mum's. My breath caught.

"She knows," Patrick whispered, eyes glinting with unshed tears. "Somehow, she knows she's part of something bigger."

He kissed my temple, both of us crying now. "What do you want to call her?"

I looked at our little girl, her tiny fingers curling around my necklace. "Her middle name… I want to use Mum's. Bella."

Patrick smiled, still watery-eyed. "Then I'd like to add my mum's. Grace."

"Grace Bella," I whispered. "Welcome to the world, baby girl."

Sienna leaned in, smiling through her own tears. "She's perfect. You guys… you did it."

She squeezed my shoulder, kissed Patrick's cheek, and stepped out to tell Travis.

The three of us were left alone—me, Patrick, and Grace. My body ached. My soul soared.

I leaned over and kissed Patrick softly. "I'm so in love with you."

"I'm in awe of you," he whispered back.

I felt warm down there—not the sexy kind of warm. The "my vagina just delivered a baby" kind of warm.

Inferno might've been closer to the truth.

When Grace was settled and safe in Patrick's arms, I waddled to the bathroom for a shower. Blood ran down my legs. My breasts were the size of balloons. My stomach looked like a deflated beach ball.

And tears? Yep. Still flowing.

The water hit my face as I stood under the spray, trying to breathe again, trying to grasp what had just happened.

The door creaked open, and I looked up.

Patrick stood there, holding a towel, his eyes sweeping over me—not with pity, not with hesitation, but like I was art—art-unfinished, powerful, raw—and he was lucky just to witness it."

As if somehow I was more beautiful now, standing barefoot in a puddle of blood and water, then I'd ever been before.

For a long second, he didn't speak. Just breathed.

Then he stepped forward and wrapped the towel gently around my shoulders, like I was made of something fragile and sacred all at once.

When his arms came around me, I let them. I needed them. "Hey, gorgeous," he whispered, voice thick.

My tears came again—this time not from pain, but from love. Fierce, messy, aching love.

The kind that strips you bare and rebuilds you in the same breath.

The kind that stays.

Just like us.

Patrick helped me get dressed and comfortable in bed, as comfortable as I could be.

Later, after the nurse checked in and Grace was safely snuggled in her bassinet, Patrick sat back in the chair in the corner of the room. He looked completely wrecked, in the best way. He ran a hand over his face, yawned, and closed his eyes.

A soft knock on the door was followed by Sienna slipping into the room, a huge smile on her face and a little container of food in her hand.

"Don't hate me, but you look like shit," she said gently, walking over to me.

"Thanks," I muttered. "I feel worse."

She leaned down, picked up Grace, and rocked her softly in her arms. "Jesus Christ, Luce. You just pushed a human out of your vagina. Do you even realise what you've done? I mean… I watched the whole thing and I still don't believe it."

I gave a tired, half-laugh. "Yeah. My vagina is going to need therapy."

She gasped, then burst into laughter. "Do you think it'll ever be the same again?"

I raised an eyebrow. "I guess I'll find out in six weeks when Patrick gets to visit it again."

A quiet snort came from the corner.

We both whipped our heads around. Patrick was sitting up in the chair now, eyes open, grinning.

"I was trying to sleep," he said. "But apparently my ears were summoned."

I groaned, burying my face in my hands. "How long were you awake?"

"Long enough to know your vagina is a hot topic of conversation," he said with a laugh. "And for the record—it'll always be perfect. Doesn't matter how many babies it pushes out."

Sienna cackled. "Well damn. That man deserves a medal." Grace let out a little coo from Sienna's arms.

The room was filled with warmth, not just from the heat, or the exhaustion, or even the shared laughter, but from the overwhelming sense that this was it.

This was life now. Messy. Loud. Beautiful.

Mine.

Ours.

Chapter 29

Welcome To The World

Coming home felt surreal.

The car ride was quiet—Grace sleeping peacefully in her seat, Patrick holding my hand the entire way. My body ached in a dozen places I didn't know could ache, but my heart?

It felt full. Overflowing, even.

When we pulled into the driveway, I saw the balloons before we even reached the door.

Jill and Joe had gone all out—soft pastel banners that read Welcome to the World, Grace Bella, ribbons wrapped around the front gate, and little flower pots lining the porch with tiny pink bows tied to each stem. The front steps were sprinkled with rose petals. The kind of welcome that said you are loved before a single word was spoken.

"I might cry again," Patrick whispered, voice catching.

I was already wiping at my eyes, the lump in my throat too big to swallow.

Inside, a small table had been set up with cupcakes, lemonade, and a few carefully chosen gifts from Jill, Joe, and Sienna. Sienna was already in the kitchen, popping mini quiches into the oven like she lived there.

"About time!" she called. "We thought you'd stopped for cocktails!"

The next hour passed in a blur of hugs, laughter, gentle cuddles of Grace, and the most comforting welcome we could've asked for. It didn't feel like a party. It felt like home had wrapped its arms around us.

When Grace began fussing, I excused myself upstairs to the nursery. Patrick and Sienna followed, falling into step behind me like shadows I never wanted to lose.

The room felt different now.

Real.

Grace's cot was no longer just furniture—it was her bed. The little bunny mobile spun lazily overhead, casting soft shapes on the wall, and Patrick's mum's blanket lay across the armchair like it had always belonged there.

I settled in to feed her, sinking into the chair as if my body knew exactly what to do.

My milk had well and truly come in, and Grace latched on like a natural. A quiet sigh escaped me.

Sienna flopped down on the rug in front of us, tossing a ball of lint at Patrick like a bored teenager.

"So, Patrick," she said, smirking, "have you tasted it yet?"

He blinked. "Tasted what?"

She deadpanned, "Her boobs, silly. Her boob milk."

Patrick's face flushed red, and he laughed awkwardly. "Uh, no. No, I haven't."

Sienna raised an eyebrow. "Well, now I'm disappointed in you."

She got up and wandered off to the bathroom, humming something suspiciously like a dramatic soap opera theme.

Grace finished feeding just as Patrick looked at me, brows lifted, lips twitching.

"Can I… try it?"

I stared at him. "Seriously?"

He gave me that crooked, charming smile—the one that always got him his way. "I'm curious. Can't hurt, right?"

I sighed, half-laughing. "Fine. But don't ruin it for yourself."

He knelt in front of me, moving with surprising reverence. But when his lips met my nipple, he clearly overcommitted.

One strong suck- and one very unfortunate squirt of milk.

He pulled back, coughing like he'd been sprayed with pepper spray—just as Sienna walked back into the room.

She stopped dead in her tracks. Eyes wide. Mouth open.

Then she clapped both hands over her face and squealed. "I was gone for sixty seconds! How is it?!"

Patrick looked like a kid caught sneaking the last cookie at a family memorial.

"Uh… good," he said weakly. "Really good. No wonder

Grace is addicted."

I tucked myself back in, laughing so hard I nearly peed.

Sienna dropped to the floor, wheezing through her laughter. "You guys are sick," she said, tears forming in her eyes.

"And proud of it," I said, kissing Grace's tiny head as she dozed off again, a little milk drunk and utterly perfect.

For a while, we just stood there—me, Patrick, Sienna—watching over the baby who had already changed everything.

The room was quiet but full. A new kind of silence. A sacred one.

Then we headed downstairs, laughter following behind us like a ribbon of light.

The world hadn't changed.

But ours had.

Grace Bella was home.

And her arrival?

It was a moment I'll never forget.

About The Author

I began my career in the hairdressing industry, where I spent years building relationships, listening to people's stories, and learning how to connect on a personal level. Eventually, I took a leap into the school education system, where I worked with young people and found purpose in helping them grow and learn. After becoming medically retired, I found myself at a crossroads and that's when I returned to something I've loved since my early teens: writing.

I live in Australia with my wonderful husband, and together we have a beautifully blended family of six children. Our home is filled with equal parts laughter, chaos, and unconditional love. Family is everything to me, and one of my greatest joys is travelling together. From ancient cities to tropical beaches, we've explored many incredible places and are always dreaming about our next adventure.

Writing this book has been both an amazing and deeply personal journey. It challenged me, inspired me, and reminded me of the healing power of storytelling. I'm incredibly proud to be sharing this story with you and hope it touches your heart in the same way writing it has touched mine.

www.ingramcontent.com/pod-product-compliance
Lightning Source LLC
Chambersburg PA
CBHW040526170726

48295CB00012B/347